WRITTEN WITH LOVE, SURROUNDED BY WAR

The Epic Story of Lady Savannah & Lord Wesley, from the Trenches to the Gilded Age

By

Harrison Vale

Print Format 5.5 x 8.5

Published by Vale House Publishing

Cover design © 2025 Vale House Publishing

Interior design and formatting by Vale House Publishing

Print - ISBN 979-8-9938340-0-9

E-Book - ISBN 979-8-9938340-1-6

Audio Book - ISBN 979-8-9938340-2-3

First Edition, 2025

VALE HOUSE
PUBLISHING

Dedication

To my beautiful Savannah, whose heart has always lived among books, and whose love has been the truest story I will ever know.

Every word that follows was written in the quiet hope that these pages might bring you the same joy you have given me in every chapter of our lives together.

Happy Anniversary.

Author's Introduction

Concerning the Crosington and Langdon Families—Their Titles, Their Power, and the Love That Bridged a World at War

At the glittering height of England's Edwardian twilight—just before the world tilted into chaos—two of the Empire's most esteemed families held court at the intersection of wealth, honour, and national influence.

On one side stood The Honourable Crosington Family, headed by His Grace, the Duke of Westford, who commanded not only the sprawling Crosington Steel & Rail Consortium, but a longstanding seat in the House of Lords, where policy and profit often met. His eldest son and heir, Sir Wesley Anderson Crosington, though not yet knighted in the formal sense, was already regarded as a rising force among England's younger elite. At just twenty-two, he was schooled at Eton and Cambridge, groomed for matters of Parliament, trade, and empire. He was expected to continue the Crosington legacy of serving both Crown and country—in commerce, politics, and war.

Opposite them stood the venerable Langdon Family of Bristol, publishers to the Kingdom and custodians of the fourth estate. Mr. William "Bill" Langdon, a baron of ink and intellect, was a confidant of ministers and magnates alike. He served on multiple royal advisory councils, helped draft policies of public influence, and, through the Langdon Press, shaped much of the British reading public's understanding of empire, diplomacy, and war. His daughter, Lady Savannah Langdon, though not titled in the peerage by blood, was nevertheless a fixture of London society. Raised amidst publishing salons and aristocratic balls, she was known for her mind as much as her manner, a woman both admired and sought after in every drawing room of distinction.

It was expected, almost fated, that Sir Wesley and Lady Savannah would one day unite their houses—not merely in marriage, but in a dynastic alliance of steel and words, of infrastructure and intellect. Indeed, the families had shared years of friendship and mutual enterprise, with whispers of an engagement stirring throughout London. Wesley and Savannah had courted discreetly, tenderly—seen strolling along the Embankment or speaking quietly in the corners of soirées. And just as

Wesley had summoned the courage to ask for her hand, war intervened.

In August of 1914, the world erupted into the flames of the Great War. Honour, legacy, and duty demanded that Wesley—like all Crosington men before him—take up arms. He joined the Royal Wiltshire Rifles and shipped out to the Western Front. The night before he left, he pressed a letter into Savannah's hands. It would be the first of many.

What follows is their story and those letters.

Written with trembling fingers in the trenches and ink-stained hands in London, these pages trace the arc of their lives through the storm of war. They speak of love restrained, of duty upheld, of family secrets buried across the sea, and of a world reshaped by sacrifice. Together, Wesley and Savannah navigate the theatre of war and the drawing room of power—each day forging a future out of memory and mud, out of longing and letters.

This is their story. A love written across continents, framed by the grandeur of the Gilded Age and the heartbreak of a world at war.

And so it begins.

CHAPTER I

OCTOBER THE 3RD, 1914
SOMEWHERE IN NORTHERN FRANCE

My Dearest Miss Savannah Langdon,

How strange it feels to hold a pen again, knowing the hand that guides it is stained with earth, and smoke, and the rusted scent of war. And yet, how deeply comforting it is to press my thoughts upon this page, as though by ink and longing I might send a part of myself across the sea to you.

It is the third day of October, and already autumn has wrapped herself about the countryside like an old shawl—soft in colour but frayed at the edges. I am writing from a small dugout no larger than the pantry at the hunting lodge. The roof leaks. The rats are ambitious.

And still, I would not trade it for a ballroom, if only because I can write to you from it in quiet.

Our company is now some ten miles from the front. We move under orders, though none of us yet understand the greater design. The lads are in good spirits, considering the circumstances. Corporal Bexley has already attempted to construct a makeshift billiards table from ammunition crates. I suspect his aim is more symbolic than recreational, but it serves to remind us that we are still men, not merely machines in muddy coats.

Do you remember, Savannah, that long walk through Hyde Park last spring? When the cherry blossoms performed their delicate descent, and we stood beneath them like characters out of one of your father's novels? You wore that pale blue dress with the mother-of-pearl buttons—the one that made the sunlight chase you down the path. I would give anything to return to that hour. To the sound of your laugh as I misquoted Byron and tripped over your parasol. I am quite certain the geese found it more poetic than you did.

There are things I long to tell you—truths I've only recently begun to face. But I fear they must wait. Not for secrecy, but for the perfect moment. I carry with me a small envelope, addressed in my own hand, sealed with the Crosington crest. It contains something I have not yet spoken of, not even to my sisters. One day, I hope to place it in your hands myself.

And speaking of my sisters, Amiee-Elizabeth and Jennifer remain as industrious as ever, writing often and sending parcels of things I never knew I needed: socks stitched with scripture, jars of Dundee marmalade, and a rather dubious collection of wartime poetry from the local ladies' society. I do not dare read the verses aloud for fear of losing the respect of my men.

Please give my warmest regards to your father, William—"Bill," as mine always called him. I recall how often they collaborated, transporting his printed materials along our railway line, turning quiet towns into informed ones with each load of inked truth. It is a bond I have only now come to appreciate fully.

But you, Savannah—you remain close to me. Closer than breath.

Write when you can. Tell me of London, of the changing leaves in Kensington Gardens, of what colours you've chosen for your gloves this season. Anything and everything. It is all gold to me.

Yours, with every beat of my soldier's heart,

Wesley A. Crosington

Private, 3rd Battalion, Royal Wiltshire Rifles

CHAPTER II

OCTOBER THE 17TH, 1914
A FIELD TENT NEAR ARTOIS, FRANCE

My Dearest Miss Savannah Langdon,

It has rained without pause for three days now. The kind of rain that mocks umbrellas and penetrates oilcloth, turning even the stiffest uniform into a sodden sack. We are mud to the knees, mud in the tea, and Bexley awoke this morning to find a frog curled in his helmet. He named it Rupert and tried to promote it to corporal. The war continues to unravel all sense of order.

I watched a sunrise this morning with Thistle, our goat. Yes, we've adopted a goat. Or rather, she adopted us. The men discovered her wandering near an abandoned farmstead, fearless as a Highlander and twice as stubborn. She has taken a particular liking to my greatcoat, and though she eats nearly everything—including Bexley's tobacco—I believe she

10

has become the soul of our little company. I suspect she outranks me now.

The rain here does not fall—it seeps. It crawls into our boots, our bread, and our bones. And yet your words have warmed me far better than any fire. I imagined you writing them by the window, your ink bottle trembling on the sill as a London fog curled in the streets below. Did you smile as you penned my name? I dare to hope you did.

The men speak of an advance soon. The whispers come through in the dark, passed like contraband between shivers. No one knows exactly when, but our boots are lined, our rifles cleaned, and the cards played slowly—drawn more from habit than heart.

Bexley is in fine form. He has fashioned a tea set from discarded shell casings and insists on serving breakfast with an accent he claims is Scottish, though I suspect it hails from the theatre more than the Highlands. He asked me to tell you that should we both survive this war, he would very much like to meet "the lovely Langdon lass."

There is something I must confess, Savannah. I have begun to dream of home—not just the house or the estate or even the hills behind Crosington Wood—but of a particular window in London, behind which I imagine

11

you reading these very words. I dream of a day not so very distant when I shall knock upon that door with dust still on my boots and ask for a glass of water—and your hand, if you'll have it.

Of course, I speak in metaphor. My courage in battle is growing, but when it comes to you, I am still that trembling schoolboy who spilled jam on your gloves at the garden fête.

I still carry the sealed envelope I mentioned. Within it is a map—a riddle, really—that speaks of a place far from here, in America no less, where something of great value waits. My father entrusted it to me before I boarded the ship to France. "One day," he said, "when the dust has settled and your heart is ready, you'll know what to do." I believe that day will come, Savannah. And I believe you are meant to find it with me.

For now, I must return to my duties. We are to dig new trenches tonight, and there are whispers of incoming gas shells. I will not frighten you with details, only assure you that we are prepared. I wear the charm you once gave me—Saint George, was it?—around my neck. It has yet to let me down.

Send news of home when you can. I long for it.

Yours in warmth, in wonder, and in whispered prayers,

Wesley A. Crosington

Private, 3rd Battalion, Royal Wiltshire Rifles

CHAPTER III

NOVEMBER THE 2ND, 1914
ENCAMPMENT NEAR BÉTHUNE

My Dearest Miss Savannah Langdon,

I write to you this evening beneath a sky the colour of tarnished pewter, with the flicker of oil lamps throwing shadows long and strange across the canvas of our tent. The days grow shorter, the nights longer, and yet your letters are the only light I truly seek. I hope that soon they arrive, like a spring breeze into a frostbitten world.

We have been in position near Béthune for near a fortnight. Our duties have shifted—now less marching and more mud. Digging, fortifying, waiting. Always the waiting. I now understand what the old colonels mean when they speak of "the silence before the storm," for silence has weight. It presses against your ribs and hums behind your eyes.

This morning, one of the lads—young Finley from Durham—asked if England had forgotten us. I told him no, that London still beat with pride, that the factories

14

hummed and the post still came, and that somewhere, someone was knitting a scarf with his name on it. It wasn't entirely untrue. You knit, do you not? You could knit a thousand scarves and never exhaust your kindness.

Thistle the goat continues to defy all military logic. She has taken up with the quartermaster's wagon and has been caught three times sleeping atop the crates of biscuits. The men now refer to her as "General Thistle." She eats like a horse, but she makes the lads laugh, and I daresay that's more valuable than the biscuits.

A strange thing happened two nights ago. I found myself walking just beyond the trench line, beneath the stars, and I caught sight of something glinting in the dirt. It was a child's marble—glass, blue and green, polished by time. It must have been lost before the war, before the land was torn open and laced with wire. I picked it up, and for a moment, I imagined it belonged to a child who once lived here, who played in these fields when they still held wheat instead of sorrow.

I keep that marble in my breast pocket now, beside your photograph.

Savannah, I must speak again of the secret I hinted at in my last letter. The object my father entrusted to me is not merely sentimental—it is valuable, though not in coin or title. It is, rather, a legacy. A key to something he built long before I knew its purpose. It lies not in England, but across the sea. Beneath a tree, behind an old red structure, hidden under the floorboards, in the land of promise. New York, he said—but not the city. Farther out, where the wind meets timber and rail, and the soil is soft with memory.

He called it a gift for the future. "For you and for her," he said. He meant you.

When this is over—when this madness ends and the flags are folded—I shall take you there, if you'll come. Together, we will unearth what he left for us. I know not what we shall find, but I know it is meant to be found together.

Until then, I remain yours, in steadfast hope and ever-deepening affection,
Wesley A. Crosington
Private, 3rd Battalion, Royal Wiltshire Rifles

November the 12th, 1914
Langdon House, Knightsbridge, London

My Dearest Wesley,

Your letters arrived like a warm firelight on the hearth after a long walk through winter fog. All three arrived at once, it must have been due to the difficulty of getting messages across the pond. I sat with them in the drawing room, letting the candle burn low as I read them—twice, in fact—and again the next morning, just to be certain your words were not dream-born. You cannot know what comfort they bring to me, nor how I cling to every detail, however small, as one would to pearls strung from memory.

I can see it now—the tarnished pewter sky you described, the faint glow of oil lamps, the laughter of men over a misbehaving goat named Thistle (General Thistle, rather—I beg her pardon). I was so moved by the image of her roosting upon the quartermaster's biscuits that I laughed aloud and startled poor Mrs. Pendergast, who was dusting the vase by the corridor. She nearly dropped it.

Dearest, your words carry more than news; they carry your soul, and in this time of so many uncertainties, that is no small thing.

London is... changed. The city hums still with industry and obligation, but there's a tension beneath it all, like a taut wire stretched just beyond its strength. The gentlemen at the club speak in clipped tones about positions and telegrams, while the ladies have adopted patriotism like a fashion. I daresay I've seen more Union Jacks sewn to gowns this season than pearls.

I attended a fundraiser hosted by Lady Wetherby last week, where titled women wrapped bandages and drank champagne with equal vigour. It is a strange world. Bethany insists that if one must stitch linen for the wounded, one might as well do so in silk gloves. And Kimberly, bless her, keeps volunteering to paint signs but forgets she cannot spell 'ambulance' without assistance. Still, I treasure these moments of levity—they are rare as silver in coal, and they make the weight of absence slightly easier to bear.

You asked if I knit—of course I do, though I dare say my creations are often more lump than loop. I shall take your request seriously, however, and begin a scarf for Finley of Durham. If the post allows, I'll send it to you for delivery, and you may tell him it was knit with stubborn affection and a good deal of accidental purling.

And Wesley—your marble. That glint of colour amid the ruin. I cannot express how that image moved me. How the past persists, even in the muck and the mire. I imagine the child who lost it, the field as it once was, and I feel such longing for peace I fear my chest may burst. I am glad you kept it. It will remind you of gentler things when the world forgets to be gentle.

As for your secret...

I knew from the start that your father was a man of mystery and meaning. That he entrusted something so sacred to you, something intended for you and I—that takes my breath away. I think often of that far land you describe, New York but not New York. A place with trees, and soil, and something hidden beneath a red building's floorboards. It sounds like the setting of a fairy tale. I do not care what the object is, my darling. The gift is you. The adventure is us.

I shall wait, Wesley. For peace, for you, for whatever your father left for us.

Come home safe.

Ever yours,

Savannah Langdon

Outside Kensington - A Cold November

Savannah Langdon sat at her desk in the blue morning light, surrounded by ink wells, blotting paper, and the faint ticking of the grandfather clock. Outside, Knightsbridge bustled with a confusion of hansom cabs and motorcars, while the milkman whistled a haunting little air that reminded her of Devon. She was calm in body but afire in mind, the kind of anxious elation that only comes when one loves someone very far away.

London society had taken on a peculiar shape in recent weeks. War had turned the city's tempo to a new and somber rhythm. Theatres remained open, but the laughter was thinner. Society balls now ended with patriotic toasts. Even the food—once flamboyant—now bore the austerity of duty. No one dared to indulge too visibly, and every noble household had turned at least one parlour into a packing room for knitted socks, tinned sardines, and letters of encouragement to the front.

Savannah kept up a brave face at these gatherings. She had her dear friends to lean upon—Bethany, ever the realist, sharp-tongued and loyal to the bone; and Kimberly, whose dramatic flair brought moments of absurd comedy that saved Savannah from despair more than once. Just last Tuesday, Kimberly had organized a "mock hospital tea" in her mother's drawing room and tried to bandage the family terrier, who was having none of it.

But under the mirth was something deeper. Savannah missed Wesley terribly. She wrote to him daily, though not all the letters were sent. Some she simply folded into a wooden box beside her bed—letters about dreams, about their future house (which she imagined wrapped in ivy), and about the names of children they might one day have.

Her heart was tethered not only to her love but to her family. Her father, William Langdon—known as "Bill" among his American publishing peers—had grown busier with each passing day, now in constant correspondence with foreign dignitaries, printers, and shipping agents. There was talk of a transatlantic partnership—something involving railway transport and the Allied propaganda effort. He was often away on business, leaving Savannah to manage many of the estate's affairs and oversee portions of the printing house's London operations.

And then there was her brother, William Pepperday Langdon. Though she hadn't seen him in weeks, he had sent a letter—brief but bursting with excitement. He had been selected for a special division of the armed forces, something unspoken but clearly elite. "Tell no one," he wrote. "But I'm going where the real work happens. Deep, dark, and dangerous." It was classic Pepper—brave, mischievous, and daring as the day was long. Savannah thought of the times they played by the river as children, Pepper pretending to be a general, her the reluctant nursemaid to his imaginary wounded.

She missed him too.

But Savannah held herself with the grace taught to her by her mother and refined by society. She knew the world was watching—London had a long memory and little mercy for women who wilted in the face of duty. So she pressed on, in lace gloves and silk skirts, writing love letters in secret and knitting scarves in stubborn hope.

Somewhere in France, her beloved was keeping a marble in his pocket, and that was enough.

At least for now.

CHAPTER IV

NOVEMBER THE 17TH, 1914
ENCAMPMENT, WESTERN FRONT

My Dearest Miss Savannah Langdon,

Your last letter arrived bundled in brown twine and wrapped in lavender-scented paper, which caused no small stir amongst the postal detail. Bexley declared it "an omen of beauty," and proceeded to wave it like a battle standard until I relieved him of his theatrical nonsense and read it—twice—under the low-hanging lantern in my dugout. I have since folded it and placed it beside your photograph and that little glass marble I told you of. The three now form my most treasured possessions.

Life at the front has become both dull and dreadful in equal measure. There are hours when nothing stirs but wind and whispers, and then—suddenly—a shell comes crashing like thunder through a church window, and we are reminded how thin the veil is between life and what lies beyond.

Yet amidst the mud, we make what joys we can. We held a "concert" of sorts last Sunday. Corporal Bexley played the harmonica—terribly, I might add—while Sergeant Emery read from a tattered volume of Shakespeare with all the subtlety of a prizefighter. I recited Wordsworth, though the men insisted it sounded more like I was reciting a recipe for goose pie. Even Thistle, our ever-steadfast goat, bleated along during the finale, which I daresay brought the house (or tent) down.

There is something in this shared struggle, Savannah, that binds us more than blood. I've begun to understand the strength of men not in their muscle or medals, but in how they hold one another upright when everything seems lost. Bexley—who once fancied himself too refined for mud—is now a lion in the trenches. He covers the younger lads like a brother, and though he still quotes poetry at odd hours, there is steel beneath his charm.

I must confess, I've grown closer to the men than I ever imagined I would. Not just as fellow soldiers, but as something akin to kin. When I lie awake at night, listening to the frost tickle the canvas and the distant boom of enemy shells, I think not just of home, but of them—my band of unshaven, sleep-deprived, biscuit-hoarding brothers.

And yet, always, I think of you. Your words have become the rhythm of my days. I can still picture the way your hand curls around your teacup, the way your lips purse in thought before you speak. I hear your laughter in the wind sometimes—though perhaps that is wishful madness.

As for the secret I carry, I feel it draw nearer in my thoughts. I have read over the note my father left me a dozen times. It speaks of a place—*our place*, he called it—in America, nestled near the edge of a wooded parcel, where the air is sweet and the soil ripe for dreams. He hid something there beneath a red barn, under the floorboards, beside a great oak tree. I do not yet know what, only that it was meant for a future that includes you.

I wonder if you've ever thought of such things—of us, together, not simply walking along the Embankment or dancing at the Hall, but truly building a life? One with roots. One with secrets to uncover and joys to claim. When I return—God willing—we shall go there, hand in hand.

For now, I must close. There is a chill tonight, the kind that climbs into your bones. But I have your letter, and in that, I have warmth enough.

Always yours,

Wesley A. Crosington

Private, 3rd Battalion, Royal Wiltshire Rifles

November the 24th, 1914
Langdon House, Knightsbridge, London

My Dearest Wesley,

Your most recent letter found me seated by the parlour window, watching the fog stretch like pale gauze across the lawn. When Cook brought in the post, I recognized your hand at once and felt my heart leap in that curious mixture of joy and ache that I believe only love—and war—can create.

I read it once by the window, again after luncheon, and once more before retiring. If it were possible to press your voice into paper, I believe I heard it then, in the rise and fall of every phrase. I laughed—yes, aloud—at the thought of dear Bexley wielding my scented letter like a knight's banner. What a picture! And your little concert—Wordsworth and Shakespeare and bleating Thistle—might've drawn more delight than the latest production at the Palace Theatre. I daresay I'd have paid handsomely for a ticket.

It comforts me beyond measure to hear how close you've grown to the men. I often imagined the trenches as a place of such solemnity that all levity was crushed beneath it, yet your words offer glimpses of firelight amidst the dark. You write of brotherhood with such tenderness, I cannot help but feel they are already part of my life—through you. Tell Bexley I shall begin composing a poem in his honour, should he ever return that harmonica.

Darling, when you speak of the land your father left—"our place," he called it—something inside me stirs like music half-remembered. I close my eyes and try to picture it: the red barn, the floorboards worn by time, the oak tree bending gently in the wind. I see us there. I do. I imagine you laying your coat over the threshold like some country squire, and me insisting it's entirely unnecessary while secretly adoring every gesture.

I do think of us, Wesley. Not simply as we are now—framed in letters and memory—but as we may be. Together. Living. Not surviving, but thriving. Raising chickens, perhaps (though Thistle might protest), and filling our cupboards with books and jam jars and small, beautiful arguments about nothing at all. I think of you building fences, cursing your hammer, and of me watching from the porch with flour on my cheek and ink on my apron. It is a dream, perhaps, but one I carry like a talisman.

Here in London, society continues with its odd mixture of bravado and denial. Bethany, Kimberly, and I attended a war relief tea hosted by the Duchess of Marlborough. There was an auction for an officer's sword—never used, thank heavens—and Kimberly bid so recklessly on a set of porcelain bandage jars that we had to restrain her. "They're simply darling," she declared, "and may be very useful when I open a pretend hospital in my drawing room."

Bethany has taken to writing limericks on donation envelopes. Her most recent reads:

"For soldiers so brave and gallant,
Give your gold or your least useful talent.
If you've no coin to spare,
Send socks, not hot air—
Or we'll know you're quite morally valiant."

She is irrepressible.

Write again soon, my love. And keep the marble close. And the photograph. And the knowledge that, though we are miles apart, we remain as near to one another as breath to a candle's flame.

Yours, with all my heart,
Savannah

Friends in the Cold

The days were growing shorter in London, and Langdon House had begun to take on that hushed, golden quality only found at the start of a long English winter. The great windows, draped in velvet, allowed in shafts of light so pale they seemed to blush before touching the floor. In that stillness, Savannah Langdon moved with purpose—organising charity drives, overseeing deliveries to the family's printing offices, and writing letters she would read a hundred times over.

In the absence of Wesley, her love had not waned but instead matured like port in a warm cellar. She no longer sighed beneath portraits or wandered aimlessly through the gardens as she had in the early weeks of the war. No, now she channelled her longing into action. She had taken up the task of managing the family's London print division with remarkable acumen. Her father, Bill Langdon, had remarked more than once that she possessed "an editor's mind in a duchess's body."

At her side were her companions, Bethany and Kimberly. Bethany, practical and pithy, had taken it upon herself to lead the society ladies in producing "morale kits"—boxes stuffed with knitted socks, peppermint humbugs, miniature hymnals, and clippings of Gilbert and Sullivan lyrics. Kimberly, ever theatrical, insisted on including a lock of her hair in each package "for bravery."

There were lighter moments too. Once, in a moment of whimsy, they painted a moustache on the bust of Queen Victoria in the drawing room and took turns speaking in exaggerated baritones. Mrs. Pendergast was horrified. Savannah nearly cried laughing.

And beneath all of this, the Langdon family remained woven into the great tapestry of wartime London—noble but restless, patriotic but weary. Bill Langdon had spent his recent days travelling between government offices and shipyards, coordinating logistics with other publishing heads. He and William Crosington had once dreamt of uniting ink and iron, rail and press—a dream not forgotten, though quieter now.

Savannah's heart remained focused across the sea, through mud-soaked trenches and dim dugouts, where her Wesley—her brave, poetic, biscuit-hoarding Wesley—carried a marble and a photograph and the future they both believed in.

And soon, she thought, they would build it. Together.

CHAPTER V

DECEMBER THE 4TH, 1914
NORTHERN FRANCE – SOUTH OF YPRES

My Dearest Miss Savannah Langdon,

How strange and marvellous it is that your letter should arrive on the very morning we stood to witness the dawn over a field that—only days ago—had been thunder and fire. The sky was quiet today, pale and aching, and your handwriting—your unmistakable script—brought more comfort than any sunbeam or song.

We have been near Ypres these last weeks, and though I am not yet allowed to say much, I will write to you honestly, as always. What we faced was not merely an engagement—it was a crucible. The Germans pushed hard through the Menin Road area, and we were among the units holding the line in that muddy, bloodied theatre. The fields here have turned to soup, thick with iron and history. I am told they call this the First Battle of

Ypres, though we men have taken to calling it *The Stubborn Stand*. And stubborn we were.

We lost many good lads. Some we buried in haste. Others we could not reach. Yet through the hail of machine fire, through the haunting shriek of shells, our spirits somehow remain intact—frayed, perhaps, but unbroken. That, I believe, is the British way. We do not always understand the shape of the world, but by God, we hold our corner of it.

It is during moments such as these that men show their true fibres. I'd like to tell you a bit more about Bexley—not the dramatic poet with the cravat and crooked smile you've imagined, but the man beneath.

Corporal Isaac Bexley comes from Kent, the son of a widowed schoolteacher who raised him and three sisters with little more than a box of Shakespeare plays and a stubborn refusal to starve. Bexley was offered a scholarship to Cambridge but turned it down when his mother fell ill. He worked as a clerk in a solicitor's office, quietly paying bills and tutoring local children in the evenings. When war broke out, he joined not out of glory or grandeur, but out of a quiet, practical sense of duty.

Here, in the mud and madness, he has become our glue. It was Bexley who pulled Private Alders from a collapsed trench during the second week at Ypres, even after his own foot had been crushed under timber. He refused evacuation. "I shan't let Jerry have all the fun," he said, grinning through the pain. He carries a small leather-bound copy of *King Lear* in his breast pocket and sometimes reads it aloud by lantern light, as if Lear's madness somehow makes our own more bearable.

Thistle the goat, ever the war's least expected mascot, survived the shelling entirely unbothered. She appeared after the chaos with a leaf stuck to her ear and a very cross expression, which Bexley insisted was her way of reminding us she disapproves of war. She is now the *Official Inspector of Tinned Goods* and has taken to headbutting anything that smells remotely edible.

I've not forgotten the secret I carry—the letter, the map, the hidden treasure buried beneath an old red structure in America. I held the envelope in my hands last night and reread my father's final note within. It speaks of a location in New York, just beyond the settled edges, where oak trees bend like dancers and a barn once stood proud against the horizon. He wrote of a cornerstone—buried deep—beneath which he placed a gift for the future. "For you, and the one who waits," he wrote.

Savannah, I do not yet know what this object is. But I know it is real. I can feel it in my bones as surely as I feel the cold steel of my rifle. I sometimes dream of it—of us standing there, on American soil, brushing the dust from the wood planks and lifting something from the earth that changes everything. I dream of your hand in mine when we find it.

We are granted a few days' rest, though the sky tells me we shan't be still long. The officers grow tenser by the hour. My own role has changed slightly—I have been tasked with tending to supplies and equipment along the northern trench routes, a small duty, but one I treat with great care. I suspect I am being watched for potential promotion, though no such word has been spoken. I take comfort in the work. It keeps the mind from drifting into dark hollows.

Please write again soon. Tell me of your father's new printing press, of the poetry readings at Covent Garden, of the colour of your hat and how you came to choose it. Tell me everything, for in your words, I find my world restored.

Yours always,

Wesley A. Crosington

Private, 3rd Battalion, Royal Wiltshire Rifles

December the 1st, 1914
Langdon House, Knightsbridge, London

My Dearest Wesley,

Your letter arrived on a morning thick with mist, the sort that makes the world feel like a dream half-forgotten. I had not even removed my gloves before tearing the seal. I pressed the pages to my lips before reading them—do forgive me for being sentimental—and then sat by the fire for an hour with only your words and the soft sound of rain against the windows for company.

What a comfort to hear that your friend Bexley bears the name Henry. I rather like it. It suits him, I think—gallant, slightly mischievous, but loyal through and through. The story of his childhood duel with the

37

pastry cart had me nearly in tears. Please tell him I admire his bravery (both past and present), and that if I ever host a fête with jam tarts, I shall have a flag in his honour.

And Emery! A solicitor's son turned sergeant—how the world reshapes us in times like these. I picture him reciting Latin phrases and then bellowing orders across muddy fields with equal fervour. There is something glorious and tragic in the way war calls men from quiet corners into roaring chapters. You must promise to return them both safely. I feel as though I know them already.

I cannot tell you how your words warm me, how they banish the ache of waiting. Your voice—though inked and folded—rings louder in my soul than the clatter of all of London. Your mention of Thistle traipsing through the munitions supply made me laugh aloud. I'm beginning to suspect that she is secretly leading the battalion.

As for the secret you carry... this place in America, this legacy your father left—each time you write of it, it feels more real. I imagine the red barn, the oak tree, the hush of forest air. It almost frightens me how deeply I want it, how much I imagine us there, a world away from gunfire and fog.

Society here continues its performance with ribbons and velvet, though the undertones grow sharper by the day. There are teas and charity concerts and formal dinners—all ostensibly for the war effort, though I sometimes wonder if some do not also enjoy the tragedy as theatre. Still, we do our part. I've become adept at organising raffles, sewing circles, and trying to coax donations from reluctant dowagers. Bethany insists on wearing military-style sashes to all events, and Kimberly, naturally, claims she is now courting an officer who once brushed shoulders with Lord Kitchener's valet. Whether he exists remains unconfirmed.

There is a tension in the air—like the taut string of a violin just before the note is played. I find myself watching the newspapers more closely now, tracing maps with my fingertip and whispering prayers over morning tea. They say things are shifting on the Continent. That the storm is coming in earnest. But I hold fast to hope, to your courage, and to the image of you reading Wordsworth by lantern light.

Come back to me, Wesley. Come back whole. And until then, keep writing. Your letters are the lifeblood of my days.

Yours always and entirely,

Savannah

Support in the Season

The winter chill had begun to settle in over Knightsbridge, curling through the alleys like an old ghost. The streets of London moved with a peculiar rhythm—half frantic, half dazed. Soldiers in uniform shared pavement with society matrons in feathered hats. Boys barely out of school ran messages while tradesmen sold brass buttons and wool socks from street carts. The war had seeped into everything. It hummed in the air like distant thunder.

Inside Langdon House, preparations for the coming holiday season had begun, albeit more muted than in years past. No great chandeliers were ordered. No imported confections arrived from France. But the silver was polished just the same, and the fires burned brightly in each room. Even in wartime, ritual clung to life like ivy on stone.

Savannah Langdon was not idle. She moved between drawing rooms and dance halls, charity auctions and committee meetings, all under the watchful eyes of London society. The daughters of peers had taken to organising everything from sock drives to social balls "in support of the troops," though the tone often veered more toward spectacle than sincerity. Still, the funds raised were real, and the socks were warm.

Bethany had appointed herself "Moral General of the Junior Committee" and carried around a notebook in which she scored each guest's donations on an invisible scale. "Lady Vellum gave only two guineas," she whispered to Savannah one afternoon, "but danced with the bandleader twice. I shall assign her a score of five out of ten." Savannah had to stifle a laugh behind her gloves.

Kimberly, on the other hand, had taken to collecting signatures of every man in uniform she met. She carried a slim blue journal with gold-trimmed pages and insisted she would bind them all into a book entitled *A Gallery of Gallant Gentlemen*. Savannah suspected most of the signatures belonged to footmen and shopboys, but Kimberly's enthusiasm was contagious.

Amid the bustle, there was always the undercurrent of uncertainty. News arrived in fragments—telegrams, whispered rumours at soirées, columns in the *Times* heavy with speculation. There was talk of battles near Ypres, of frostbite setting in on the front lines, of trains bearing wounded men through the countryside. And yet, the theatres remained open, the hats still feathered, and the dinners candlelit.

Savannah navigated these contradictions with quiet grace. She wore her finest gloves to council meetings and muddy boots to the warehouse where parcels were sorted. She smiled at lords and laboured among ladies' maids. And always—always—her thoughts drifted back to a man in a trench, somewhere beneath the pewter skies of France.

Each letter she received from Wesley Crosington was read and reread until the creases grew soft. She carried them in her coat pocket, beneath her gloves, or tucked inside her sewing basket. Sometimes she would sit alone in the garden pavilion—even in the cold—and whisper his words aloud just to hear them.

It was not a life of stillness, though it often felt paused. The world had turned upside down, but she held to the belief that love, like the stars above the city, remained constant—if only one remembered to look up.

CHAPTER VI

A SILENT NIGHT

DECEMBER THE 27TH, 1914
NEAR YPRES, BELGIUM

My Dearest Miss Savannah Langdon,

I received your latest letter this morning and, I must confess, I held it in my hands for a full five minutes before opening it. There is a particular joy—a reverence, even—that attends the unwrapping of something so personal amidst so much that is impersonal: regulation meals, government-issued boots, the endless, grey uniformity of mud. But your handwriting—so delicate and yet so strong—reminds me there is a world beyond all this, and that it waits for me. That you wait for me.

My dearest Savannah now I must tell you of a miracle too good to be true, if I had not lived it myself, I might have believed it fantasy. And yet, with my own eyes I beheld it: a night of peace in a world of war.

I write to you now not from the clamour of shells, nor from the trembling of trenches—but from a quiet morning, when the snow still rests undisturbed upon the earth and not a single shot has cracked the dawn.

We had a Christmas, Savannah. A real, true Christmas—even here.

On the eve of the 24th, there was a stillness that settled over the line like frost over a grave. The wind had fallen away, and even the rats seemed reluctant to stir. We had heard rumours—whispers from the northern sector—that the German troops had begun to sing hymns across No Man's Land.

We thought it absurd.

But then—just after dusk—our men heard it. Soft and unsure at first. But growing clearer with each verse:

"Stille Nacht, heilige Nacht..." "Silent Night, holy night..."

At once, a hush fell over our trench. Even Chuffy, whose jaw seldom pauses long enough for thought, stood as if frozen. Then, from somewhere in our line, a response—tentative, but full of feeling:

"Silent night, holy night, All is calm, all is bright..."

Voices joined in, one by one, until the entire line was echoing with that most hallowed of hymns—two armies bound in reverence, if only for a verse.

When the final note faded into the cold, a cheer arose from their side—and we answered with our own.

The morning that followed, at first light, we saw a small figure rising from the German trench, waving a white flag—not in surrender, but in invitation.

And then, astonishingly, others followed—hands held high, weapons left behind.

We looked to our officers, unsure. Even I, who am meant to lead, could scarce believe what I saw. But as no shot was fired, and no treachery revealed, our own lads began to climb out. Slowly, cautiously... and then with growing boldness.

We met in the middle of No Man's Land.

Men shook hands. Introduced themselves. Exchanged chocolates, tinned meats, cigarettes. One German had a button from a Liverpool football club; Bexley gave him a packet of tea in return. Moth handed a chap his only pair of clean socks. "Take them," he said, "my toes gave up the ghost last week."

You will laugh at this, dearest—we played football.

Yes, truly! Someone produced a makeshift ball—little more than a battered ration tin—and sides were picked with all the seriousness of a proper league match.

I served as referee, though it must be said I was bribed with a biscuit on more than one occasion.

The Germans won, 3–2.

After the football match had ended, we found ourselves standing amidst the churned fields of No Man's Land, breath fogging in the cold, and a strange quiet settling over us once more.

It was then—just past four o'clock, by my watch—that a German sergeant with wire spectacles and a heart too generous for war stepped forward, bearing a tin pot the size of a top hat. From it wafted a rich, oniony scent that made Moth declare, with solemnity, that he had not smelled a vegetable since August.

"Kartoffelsuppe," the German said, grinning. Potato soup.

Moments later, a British lad from the Leicesters returned the gesture, lifting a small wooden crate filled with cans of plum-and-apple jam, some nearly expired biscuits, and a brined ham wrapped in burlap that had been mistakenly delivered from supply the week prior. (We had intended to send it to the rear for officers, but no one could resist now.)

And so it began.

Tables were made from overturned crates and planks scavenged from ammunition boxes. Soldiers draped tattered tarps as tablecloths. One clever chap used an old shovel stuck in the mud to prop up a lantern, giving the field an eerie but almost festive glow.

From all sides came small offerings:

- The French brought red wine hidden in water flasks.

- The Scots unveiled a round of hard cheese, likely older than Titch's sense of humour.

- A German officer unwrapped a parcel from home: Lebkuchen—gingerbread baked by his mother, still bearing her handwritten note in looping script.

- Bexley contributed a treasured tin of Queen Mary's Christmas Pudding, wrapped in the royal crest. He refused to eat any, however, and instead passed it reverently around so each man could smell it, eyes closed, as if in chapel.

We made plates of boiled potatoes, tinned meat, and stale bread softened in soup. It was, by any civilised measure, a poor meal.

But I tell you now, Savannah, I have never tasted anything finer.

That afternoon, Bexley read aloud from the Gospel of Luke:

"Glory to God in the highest, and on earth peace, goodwill toward men."

A German chaplain offered a blessing in his tongue; ours followed in English. Men bowed their heads together. I saw one of our lads and a Prussian corporal weeping side by side.

It was the most sacred moment I've ever known.

During dinner, the talk was cautious at first.

I sat across from a Bavarian lieutenant named Josef, whose English was clipped but passable. He told me he had studied law in Leipzig, and had seen Shakespeare performed once in Berlin. He asked if all English women were as refined as Juliet.

I told him no, most were far more dangerous.

He laughed and replied, "Good. Then we are alike."

To his left was a Saxon soldier—barely older than Summer—who shared that he had never before seen an Englishman up close. I offered him a boiled sweet from my coat pocket. He took it with tears in his eyes and said it reminded him of his sister, who used to steal them from their village shop.

To my right, Moth was in fierce debate with a Prussian engineer over the merits of British coal vs Saxon coal. No winner was declared, but the engineer did gift Moth a carved pipe in the shape of an eagle.

After dinner, someone began to sing again.

It was "O Come, All Ye Faithful." First in Latin—Adeste Fideles—then in English. Then in German.

The snow began to fall again.

Soft, slow flakes drifted down onto the table, the soup pots, the boots of old enemies now sharing warmth from a common fire. Someone passed around a flask of schnapps. Bexley recited a bit of Kipling. Hensley tried to translate it into French, failed terribly, and accidentally insulted a Belgian who still toasted him nonetheless.

It was cold. Our hands trembled. The boots squelched in frozen mud. But in that moment, we were not soldiers.

We were simply men—sons, brothers, husbands, lovers—breaking bread in a broken world.

We shook hands again in the dark. Some men embraced. A few exchanged addresses, though we knew most letters would never pass the censors.

And then, one by one, we returned to our trenches.

The firelight faded behind us. And the stars resumed their watch.

That Christmas Eve and Day, in a land ravaged by hate and sorrow, the Prince of Peace walked among us. Not in glory, but in soup pots and broken songs, in pipe smoke and jam tins, in borrowed smiles and shivering shoulders pressed side by side.

I shall carry it with me always. And if I live to see you again, I shall tell you every word by firelight.

And then, always, I return in thought to the envelope I carry. It still sleeps in the satchel beneath my cot. My father's handwriting has faded slightly, but the words burn bright in my mind:

"To my son, and to the woman who holds his heart—what is buried here shall one day build something greater than either of you alone."

That place—it lies in New York, under the floorboards of an old red barn, beside a weathered oak, I now believe he placed with his own hands. I do not yet know what lies beneath, only that it will matter. And I know this, too: I will not open it without you.

Until then, I shall carry your letters as sacred things. I shall write you when I can, and speak to you in silence when I cannot.

With unwavering affection and the promise of return,

Wesley A. Crosington

Private, 3rd Battalion, Royal Wiltshire Rifles

January the 2nd, 1915
Montague Square, London

My Dearest Wesley,

The city sleeps beneath a blanket of pale fog this morning, the sort that clings to the windows and silences the horses' hooves upon the cobbles. It is the sort of day made for tea, for quiet musings, and for writing to you, which I do now from the small green sofa beside the hearth—the very one you once fell asleep upon with your boots shamefully propped upon one of Mother's best cushions. I have forgiven you, though I suspect the cushion has not.

Your account of Christmas at the Front moved me more than I can say. To imagine such peace in the midst of ruin — men who only hours before had fired upon one another now sharing bread and song beneath the same cold stars — it feels almost miraculous. I confess, I wept a little as I read it. There is something profoundly human in that fragile moment of grace, something that

53

makes all our prayers seem less like whispers into the dark. I am proud of you, my dearest, and proud too of every soul who dared to be kind when the world had forgotten how.

London is not untouched by the war, Wesley. Though the battles rage far from our shores, the tension curls into our drawing rooms like smoke beneath the door. Rations have begun—eggs are rarer than diamonds—and the post arrives later each day, often missing entirely. Still, life marches on, though now to a more somber beat.

Father remains tirelessly at work at the press. He's taken to printing leaflets for the Ministry—propaganda, they call it, though he insists it is merely "spirited encouragement." I fear he pushes himself too hard. His eyesight fails him in the evenings, and I often find him squinting by candlelight, murmuring about margins and headlines. You know how he becomes when an idea takes root—like a fox chasing down a chicken in his mind.

My days are spent at the hospital on Harley Street, where I assist with bandage rolling, and occasionally reading aloud to the wounded. You'd be surprised how many prefer Dickens over Shakespeare, though I suspect it's less literary taste and more the comfort of familiar old stories. I carry your photograph in my locket, and a great many nurses have asked about you. I tell them only that you are away, serving—though I suspect they imagine you a handsome cavalryman. You may thank me later for the exaggeration.

As for my friends, Bethany and Kimberly have been my saving grace. Bethany is as forthright as ever—last week, at a Red Cross luncheon, she challenged the Vicar's son on his cowardice for not enlisting. It caused quite the scandal, though privately I rather admired her for it. Kimberly, on the other hand, is softer in her rebellion. She has begun sketching again and swears she shall one day paint the war in hues no man has yet dared.

We three walk often in Hyde Park, discussing everything from courtship to corsets, and pretending the world is not falling apart. It is easier when we are together. Lately we have taken to collecting stories from wounded soldiers to publish in Father's paper—anonymously, of course. We believe people must know the truth, or at least enough of it to remind them that the men out there are more than names on a page.

I have not forgotten your secret. The idea of something hidden—waiting for us, placed by your father no less—haunts my imagination like the final act of a mystery novel. I sometimes close my eyes and try to picture it: a barn, red and weathered by rain, an oak tree older than either of us, and beneath its shade, a cornerstone that holds a future. A gift, you say. I dare not guess what it might be, only that whatever it is, it already feels like ours.

Do take care of yourself, my beloved Wesley. Be brave, yes—but be safe, too. I beg of you, do not mistake valor for recklessness. I have no use for medals if they come without you. Write soon. I remain always yours.

With all my heart,
Savannah Langdon

Longing from London

Though she would never admit it aloud, Savannah Langdon feared the silence most of all.

It crept into her nights, between the ticking of the brass carriage clock and the creaking of the old pipes in the Montague Square house. It hovered behind the chatter of charity events and the rustle of skirts at tea, waiting—always waiting—for the post that might never arrive. Each letter from Wesley brought joy, yes, but also dread—for what if it were the last?

In public, Savannah played her role. The daughter of a respected printer, she walked with grace, listened with poise, and offered balm to wounded spirits. But beneath the surface—beneath the lace gloves and perfectly pinned hair—she was a woman at war in her own right.

Bethany and Kimberly knew. They saw through the smile, heard the tremble in her voice when the topic turned to the front. They held her hand when she faltered, and together, the three women became a silent force: fundraising, printing, listening, speaking truth in coded whispers.

And yet, for all the sorrow, Savannah carried hope like a candle in the fog. A quiet, persistent flame that no bombardment could extinguish.

Written with LOVE, Surrounded by WAR

CHAPTER VII

JANUARY THE 10TH, 1915
OUTSKIRTS OF PLOEGSTEERT WOOD, BELGIUM

My Dearest Miss Savannah Langdon,

The moon was high above the wood last night, and her light—silver, solemn—cast long shadows through the bare branches of the trees. It was so still I could hear the distant whistle of a train from the east, reminding me that the world moves on, even when it feels as though we've stepped out of time. It made me think of you. Of London. Of all we have yet to see together.

The frost came early, crisping the edges of every canvas and lash. We've moved again, this time to the edges of Ploegsteert Wood, where the trees seem to whisper old stories when the wind is right. Here, for the first time in many weeks, we've been granted a lull in the fighting. Some say the Germans are regrouping. Others whisper of something worse. But I try not to listen to rumours—only to the breathing of the men around me, and the sound of my own heart, which beats still because of fortune, or Providence, or perhaps simply your love.

I want to tell you now of Private Charles Thompson, the third pillar of my little circle.

Thompson is of Scottish descent, but raised in Liverpool by a grandmother who swore the Highland blood was still thick in him. She was not wrong. He is as lean as a birch, with arms like corded rope and hair as black as a raven's wing. He does not speak often, but when he does, it is always something worth hearing.

He was once a shipwright's apprentice—he could mend a hull with nothing but bent nails and a prayer—and when war came, he left behind a fiancée named Moira, whose name he carves carefully into the heel of every pair of boots he's issued. I have seen him carry wounded men twice his size across fields so thick with mud we feared even the rats had drowned.

What makes Thompson truly singular, however, is his quiet integrity. He never raises his voice, never boasts, never shouts. But when he places his hand on your shoulder, you feel steadier. He is, perhaps, the man I trust most with my life.

We shared a moment this week—just he and I—repairing the hinges of a shattered field box. He asked about you. I told him only what I felt I could bear to say aloud—that you are the brightest thing I have ever known, and the reason I wake and march and write. He nodded and said, *"Then she must be worth all this."* I did not know how to reply. I still do not.

Thistle, by the by, has developed a taste for Belgian turnips and refuses to sleep anywhere but inside Bexley's tent. He pretends to hate it, but I suspect he finds her company more agreeable than ours. She butts at our boots each morning like a sergeant on parade.

Savannah, I have begun to dream of the thing buried beneath the red barn. I can see it sometimes—not clearly, just in feeling. It is wrapped in oilcloth and something older, something wooden, perhaps. My father wrote of it only once, and briefly. *"You will know it when you hold it, and she will understand before you do."*

The wind howls tonight. I must close. We've orders to reinforce our section at dawn. I do not know what the morrow will bring, but I know this: I am yours, utterly and always.

Ever faithfully,
Wesley A. Crosington
Private, Royal Wiltshire Rifles

January the 15th, 1915
Montague Square, London

My Beloved Wesley,

How I long to be that moon above the trees you wrote of—to shine quietly upon your path and whisper light across the dark forest of your days. Your words reach me like a warm shawl in this cold season, and I wrap myself in them greedily.

London remains unchanged and ever-changing. The streets bustle with new uniforms and old sorrows. Each day another young man boards a train, cheered by ribbons and hopeful sisters. And each day another telegram is delivered in silence. We see it in the postman's face before he even knocks.

Kimberly has begun painting a series of watercolours she calls *The Departures*—families on steps, soldiers on platforms, mothers in windows. They are heartbreakingly still. Bethany, meanwhile, has drafted her third letter to the Home Office demanding greater female involvement in wartime planning. I fear she may soon be charged with treason—or offered a Cabinet seat.

I continue at the hospital and the press. Father is training two new lads, both too young and too eager, but he believes in second chances. He says *"Type, not age, determines a man."* The work keeps me grounded, though the air hangs heavy now that your letters come weeks apart.

I think of your goat daily. Tell her I send my warmest regards.

Yours in endless thought,
Savannah Langdon

London, Reality in Winter

Savannah Langdon's days were a study in paradox: full and yet somehow hollow. She moved through them like a ghost in silk—polished and purposeful on the outside, but aching just beneath.

Each morning, she walked to the hospital on Harley Street, her boots clicking crisply on the frost-kissed pavement. There, amidst the antiseptic smell of carbolic soap and the murmurs of nurses, she rolled bandages, wrote letters for blinded soldiers, and whispered comfort to boys younger than her youngest cousin. She never asked about their wounds. She let them speak only what they chose, and in return, they told her everything: about home, about girls, about the terror of the gas and the silence afterward.

Afternoons were spent at Langdon Press, where her father stood hunched like a question mark over the rollers. The war had transformed their respectable newspaper into something greater—and more dangerous. Stories arrived by telegram and whisper, and Savannah found herself editing lines that could tilt public hope one way or the other. She wielded a red pencil like a scalpel.

At home, the social dances had changed in tempo. Where once there had been frivolous soirees and floral arrangements, now there were charity drives, auctions for the widows' fund, and tea parties that ended in whispered tears. The women of London did not stop meeting—they simply met differently.

Kimberly, ever the romantic, became quieter with each passing month. Her paintings turned darker. Bethany, by contrast, grew louder, railing against Parliament and the War Office, against the notion that courage was measured only in bullets and brass. Between them, Savannah found her compass. They were her anchor and her wings.

But it was in the quiet hours—when the city exhaled and the gaslamps flickered low—that Savannah truly struggled. The letters came less frequently. The news more grim. And though she never allowed herself to cry at the table or in the street, her pillow knew the weight of tears.

Still, she held firm. She read poetry aloud each night—sometimes to her mother, sometimes to herself. She kept Wesley's photograph beside her lamp, and on particularly hard days, she wrote him letters she never sent—lines too intimate, too fraught to put to post.

And always, always, she wondered about the secret—the gift, the thing buried in New York beneath the barn and the oak and the cornerstone. It became her talisman. When her courage faltered, she closed her eyes and imagined unearthing it with him, side by side, dirt beneath their nails and future in their hands.

That hope, more than anything else, kept her upright.

CHAPTER VIII

JANUARY THE 26TH, 1915
FORWARD LINES – NEAR
SAINT-YVES, BELGIUM

My Dearest Miss Savannah Langdon,

I write you tonight by the dim glow of a smuggled oil lamp—smuggled not by black market but by Thistle herself, who has commandeered a lantern belonging to the Quartermaster's clerk. It is now hers, by right of theft, and we dare not reclaim it, for she glares at any man who approaches. We've begun calling her *Major Thistle* behind her back.

Our unit has advanced further east, now entrenched on a ridge not far from Saint-Yves. The ground here is soaked with rain and history—every footstep squelches with the weight of lives lived and lost. Still, the trees bloom with icicles, and the frost makes even a cratered landscape shimmer in the moonlight like some alien cathedral.

You will be glad to know that I have, at last, been entrusted with command over our quarter-company's daily watch logs. It is small, clerical work to some—but to me, it is an acknowledgment of steadiness. I feel myself being shaped, Savannah—not into someone else, but into the person I was always meant to become. The boy who once fumbled his way through Latin declensions now carries the names of thirty-eight men upon his back, and I will not let them down.

Bexley and Emery remain my bookends of chaos and calm. Bexley has written a comedic opera about trench life that he insists will take London by storm once staged. I fear it includes a scene wherein Thistle plays the piano with her hooves. Emery, ever the quiet guardian, found a frozen bird this morning and buried it with the reverence of a bishop. He later told me he once wished to become a teacher, before Margaret and the mines and the war.

Each day I learn more about these men—not through grand revelations, but through their silences, their jokes, the way they clean their rifles or mend a tear in another's coat. The longer we remain here, the more I understand that the heart of war is not glory, but persistence. Not banners, but fellowship.

And yet, even in this place, you live in me.

I think of you constantly—sometimes in reverie, sometimes in ritual. I fold your letters into the inner pocket of my tunic, over my heart. I take them out on days when the guns are quiet. Yesterday, beneath a grove of ash trees, I read again your words about the oak and the cornerstone. I believe my father wrote of that tree not only because it marked the spot of the secret, but because he knew what it would mean to you.

You are rooted, Savannah—more than any woman I have ever known. The world may tremble and burn, but I know that you remain: clever, curious, composed. I know, too, that your world is not without struggle. I see it in the shape of your sentences, in the ink-blots where your hand paused in thought. I hope you know that I carry your burdens beside my own.

I dreamt last night—not of battle, but of a walk we once took in Hyde Park. You wore a dark green coat with brass buttons, and your gloves did not match, which annoyed you until I told you I liked them better that way. We stopped near the Serpentine to feed the swans, and you made up names for each one—*Viscount Beak, Lady Feathers, Archibald of the Ripples*. I laughed so hard I nearly dropped the bread. Do you remember?

In the dream, you turned and said, *"Promise me we'll laugh again."*

I do. I shall. We will.

Word from home has grown scarce. My sisters' latest note was brief—just a mention of Sir Roger hosting guests from Liverpool and a vague reference to business matters that "need attention, but nothing urgent." I know them well enough to read between the lines. Something stirs, but they will not tell me until they've already done it.

There is talk among the officers of a new offensive come spring. Some say we'll push further into Flanders. Others say we hold. I say only this: I shall go where I must, but I will always return to you. Somehow, in some fashion.

I end this letter with my boots off, my toes steaming by the fire, and Thistle snoring beside my knapsack. It is not glamour, but it is life. And it is mine, still. Because of you.

Yours in snow and fire,
Wesley A. Crosington
Acting Corporal, Royal Wiltshire Rifles

February the 1st, 1915
Montague Square, London

My Dearest Wesley,

You would have laughed to see us last night, positively frozen in our silks and foolish shoes, prancing about Grosvenor House in the name of patriotism. A charity masquerade for the Red Cross, hosted by Lady Swithenham herself—her first ball since the war began, and a most determined attempt to prove that dignity could survive in chiffon and candlelight.

Bethany came dressed as Britannia, with a papier-mâché trident and a plumed helmet that would not stay on straight. Kimberly arrived as a Greek muse, which was entirely too vague a choice, though she insisted the mystery was the point. I, feeling bold, attended as Queen Elizabeth—ruff, pearls, and all. My father snorted when he saw me and said, "The printer's daughter has become the monarch's ghost." I chose to take it as praise.

The war was not forgotten, of course—it hovered like smoke above every chandelier—but for a few hours, there was laughter, music, and dancing. It felt like breathing again.

Wesley, I have news that has left my heart both proud and anxious.

I received a letter yesterday from William—my brother, whom you may only faintly recall from our childhood summers, when he used to pester us during garden luncheons by firing imaginary pistols at the trellis. He has enlisted—no, not merely enlisted, but been accepted into a special operations unit. He wrote in cryptic phrases, of course, citing "the usual military secrecy," but I could tell he is deeply honoured. He leaves for training immediately.

Do you remember how he used to dress in your father's old greatcoat and declare himself Captain Pepperday Langdon, Defender of the Empire? We'd run along the riverbank near Clifton, he with a stick for a sword, I with a book for a shield. He once dug a trench in the garden so deep the gardener threatened to quit. It seems the boy never truly left the woods behind.

I am terrified for him, and yet... oddly comforted too. Knowing you are both out there—serving, enduring, becoming—makes this house feel less quiet and more like a listening post, catching the echoes of history.

Bethany and Kimberly have been my salvation these last few weeks. When gloom settles like a second coat, they sweep me away without warning—sometimes to sketch in the V&A Museum, other times to drink chocolate at Fortnum's as if the world were not unraveling. Bethany says we owe it to the soldiers to remain somewhat fabulous. Kimberly just likes the biscuits.

You are in my every prayer, my every quiet moment, my every breath between heartbeats. I know the winter has been cruel, and that each sunrise demands more of you than words can hold. But I also know this: the earth still turns, even in sorrow, and spring will find you.

Until then, I remain yours. Entirely.

With love that cannot be measured,
Savannah Langdon

London, February 1915

Savannah Langdon wore her grief like a silk sash—elegant, hidden, and always present. Each morning began with a ritual: the opening of the curtains (even if it was raining), the setting of tea, and the reading of the post. She lived now in rhythms, not events.

But once in a while, the city conspired to lift her.

The masquerade ball had been Bethany's idea, of course. "If we must go mad," she declared, "let us do it in velvet." Savannah had nearly declined, but Kimberly, with her soft hands and large brown eyes, had fetched a box of her mother's costume jewelry and refused to leave until Savannah chose a necklace. "You are still allowed to be dazzling," she whispered.

And so, for one night, Savannah danced.

She had forgotten how it felt to glide, to be spun across a floor like a girl in a dream. The music—a string quartet with a penchant for Vivaldi—seemed to stitch her back together, one note at a time. When she left the ballroom, her cheeks flushed and her gloves missing, she felt almost like herself again.

Then came William's letter.

It arrived on pale brown paper, folded crisply, with handwriting she had not seen in months—sharper now, more precise. He had been accepted, he said, into a newly formed reconnaissance division with special training and classified objectives. "Think of me as a shadow among the shadows," he wrote.

Savannah had wept—silently, over the sink while peeling carrots—and then told no one for a day. Not because she doubted his bravery, but because she feared her own heart could not stretch to hold two soldiers at once.

She remembered William as a boy: wild-haired, sunburnt, always in motion. He built forts from laundry baskets, declared wars on invisible foes, and insisted on being called "Sergeant Pepper" long before it was ever earned. He once leapt into the river fully clothed, declaring it a necessary ambush.

She had adored him. Still did.

And now he belonged to the world of men and maps, of missions and silence. Just like Wesley.

Her friends sensed the shift.

Bethany, all fire and indignation, began dragging her to public lectures—some dull, some electrifying.

Kimberly insisted they join the Women's Auxiliary Embroidery League, where Savannah stitched precisely one half of a floral motif before spilling tea on it.

They made her laugh. That was their gift.

In their company, Savannah forgot the war long enough to giggle at a hideous hat, or to whisper rude poetry behind fans, or to sneak off to the park with a bottle of elderflower cordial. They did not replace her sorrow, but they dulled its edges.

Each night, Savannah returned home to Montague Square, hung her coat, and stood for a moment by the fire. Her mother would be upstairs with a novel, her father at the press or asleep in his chair. The house creaked with age and memory.

And then she would write—to Wesley, to William, sometimes to no one. Her words were her tether, her weapon, her prayer.

For though she walked the halls of a quiet home, Savannah Langdon was no passive heroine. She was enduring. She was waiting. And one day, she knew, she would board a ship or a train or a carriage toward something vast and unfinished—and find them both again.

CHAPTER IX

FEBRUARY THE 13TH, 1915
ENCAMPMENT AT NEUVE
CHAPELLE, NORTHERN FRANCE

My Dearest Miss Savannah Langdon,

The wind here speaks in long vowels, echoing across the scarred woods like a low organ note in a stone cathedral. We are posted now at Neuve Chapelle, a hamlet clinging to the edge of memory and ruin. Its church is no more than a skeleton, and yet the bell still hangs, half-rung, in defiance of everything that has tried to tear it down. There's poetry in it, I think.

Rumours of an offensive are thick as the damp in our boots. We've been told to rest while we may—officers rotating, patrols lightened, hot rations served (with a rare bit of salt, which sent Thompson into what I can only call an out-of-body experience). The quiet, however, is not peaceful. It is anticipatory. Like the moment before a curtain rises—only we do not know the play, nor our roles, nor how many will exit before the final bow.

This war teaches one strange truths, Savannah. Time no longer moves forward, but outward. A single day can feel as dense as a novel, while a week can vanish like smoke. I have begun keeping a private journal, just fragments, bits of thought. Today I wrote: *"Courage is not the absence of fear, but the practice of facing it while folding your socks."*

Emery and Bexley remain my twin lighthouses—one steady, one flashing erratically in all directions. Emery has been carving small animals from discarded shell casings. He gifted me a brass hare with lopsided ears that he says reminds him of the way I run when cold. Bexley, meanwhile, insists on calling his new trench boots "the Duchess" and speaks to them before bed.

We've also adopted a new regiment goat. Her name is officially "Lady Percival Thistle VI," but we just call her *Thistle* yet again, as we are simple men here. She is terrible, bites boots, and tried to eat the edge of my greatcoat yesterday. The men adore her. She has somehow acquired a private billet in the supply tent.

We laugh more than I thought we would. It is a survival of its own kind.

As for my own standing—I find myself shouldering more without being told to. The officers nod to me more now. I am asked to speak at briefings. I've begun waking up before the bugle, not because I must, but because the men expect me to. I never thought leadership would arrive not with a shout, but with a shared look over a breakfast tin. Yet here it is, quiet and weighty.

I reread your last letter under my blanket, by the flicker of a scavenged candle stub. You spoke of the masquerade, of Bethany's trident and Kimberly's vague Grecian aspirations. I could picture it all—the absurd glory of London trying to dance through grief. It gave me such joy. I thank you for it.

Your words are a map, Savannah. They remind me not of where I am, but of where I must return.

Last night, I dreamt again of the barn.

Not the real one—no, the dream barn was grander, glowing faintly beneath a harvest moon. The oak beside it was vast, its roots like arms wrapping around something precious. In the dream, I knelt beside the cornerstone and felt the earth give way to my hand. I could not see what lay below, only that it belonged to us. Not a treasure, but a trust.

And so I carry on, letter by letter, mile by mile.

We are preparing, Savannah. For what exactly, I cannot say. But when it comes, I will stand firm—not for medals, nor glory, but for the hope that one day I will ride with you beside me again, across hills unscarred by shell or sorrow.

Yours faithfully and with growing resolve,
Wesley A. Crosington
Acting Corporal, Royal Wiltshire Rifles

February the 21st, 1915
Montague Square, London

My Most Beloved Wesley,

I read your last letter in the morning light, the one that filters through my bedroom curtains in slanted streaks, golden and uncertain. I pressed the page to my lips, as though the warmth of you might linger in the ink, and sat silently for a long while after, my heart split between pride and longing.

You speak of courage as folding one's socks in fear. I rather think mine is putting on a hat and going to luncheon with Lady Beltram, knowing full well she will ask me—point-blank—when we intend to wed. (I told her we would do so once you return, whole and victorious, and not a moment before. She sniffed and said, "Well, do hurry, dear. There's a shortage of good men and an oversupply of sentimental girls.")

London, you see, is not what it was. There is a kind of tension here, like a string pulled taut that no one dares to release. Rationing has begun in earnest. Mother and I stood in queue at the grocer's for nearly an hour last Tuesday, all for a slab of butter and two eggs. I felt quite the pioneer. Mother remarked that wartime turns the highborn into hens and the hens into delicacies.

The press is running night and day. Father is adamant that the public must not lose faith in the Empire, and I do my best to ensure the words we publish remain both honest and hopeful. It's a fine balance. Yesterday, we printed a story about a boy from Surrey who returned home with one arm and a medal. The picture shows his mother beaming. I wept while setting the type.

Bethany and Kimberly have done their best to distract me from my gloom. On Thursday, we attended a performance of *The Man Who Stayed at Home* at the Royalty Theatre—a curious spy drama that had Bethany hissing at the villain and Kimberly crying over a character's briefcase. Afterward, we found a tiny café still serving tea (with real milk!) and toasted your name with little sugared biscuits. Kimberly said you would have liked the villain better, for his cunning. Bethany said you would have knocked him out and stolen his boots. I said you would have found the playwright and offered him a better ending.

There is news, too, of William. I received a brief note from him this morning—cryptic, brave, and full of hints. He is training for something *"special and unusual,"* as he put it. I suspect it is something terribly dangerous, though he would never say so. His handwriting has grown steadier. His signature, once a scrawl, now carries the weight of a man. He asked after you, and I told him only what I know: that you remain steadfast, brave, and very much missed.

Do take care of yourself, my love. And if the goat bites you again, bite her back. That seems fair.

With all that is in me,
Savannah

London, in a Quiet February

The days had grown shorter again, but not in the usual way. Time itself seemed contracted in wartime London—rushing and halting, unsure of which season it belonged to.

Savannah Langdon stood at the centre of a city trying to smile through its mourning. The newspapers stacked in her father's printing house bore headlines that promised resolve, but the men who delivered them were growing younger by the week. She noticed that. Everyone did.

The war had aged her. Not in the face—no, she was still as fresh and clever as ever, with her dark hair piled high and her eyes wide and watchful—but somewhere inward, in the clockwork of her spirit. Her steps were surer, her words more precise. She had learned to speak plainly to frightened mothers and to laugh politely at grim jokes from politicians who mistook gallows humour for good leadership.

But she had not, and would not, surrender her joy.

Bethany and Kimberly had made it their mission to ensure that. They burst into her life like living postcards, ridiculous and golden and loud. Kimberly brought a French lipstick she had bartered from a departing soldier and insisted they all wear it to the theatre, "in honour of bravery." Bethany, ever the philosopher, had taken to reciting Shakespeare at random intervals during tea, always choosing lines with ominous resonance.

Their friendship was not frivolous—it was resistance.

Savannah clung to them. In their company, she remembered how to be young. Not naïve, but *alive*. When Kimberly painted a red stripe on her cheek and declared her "a duchess in exile," Savannah laughed so hard she spilled jam down the front of her best skirt.

And yet, in quiet moments, the weight returned.

She missed Wesley. She missed the steadiness of his gaze, the way he folded his arms when he thought hard, the sound of him tapping a pencil against the inside of his boot while reading. She missed their walks through

Kensington, the way his gloved hand found hers just as the gaslamps flickered to life.

In dreams, she saw him climbing through snow. Or walking toward her across a green field filled with crows. Sometimes he was smiling. Sometimes he was bruised. She always woke with the ache of something unfinished.

Her letters to him had grown longer.

She wrote them late at night, when the city was quietest. They were laced with longing, but also pride. She did not want to be his sorrow—only his beacon. So she filled her pages with jokes, with gossip, with hope.

And when the letter from her brother arrived—brief and coded, no return address—she did not cry, not at first. She simply held it, and whispered, "So you're going too."

She remembered the games they'd played near the Avon River—Pepper in his toy uniform, declaring war on shadows, digging trenches in the garden, making Savannah the "Minister of Spy Affairs." She had always laughed at him then.

Now she was simply afraid.

She told no one of her fear. Not even Bethany, who surely suspected. Instead, she walked to the park, sat beneath the winter-stripped willow, and read Wesley's last letter again. He had dreamt of the barn. Of the oak tree. Of a secret buried deep.

She closed her eyes and imagined them there—together, one day, standing on American soil, in a place untouched by war. A home. A future.

She would wait. She would endure. She would believe.

And until then, she would dance when invited, laugh when able, and write to him always.

CHAPTER X

MARCH THE 6TH, 1915
ENCAMPMENT OUTSIDE NEUVE CHAPELLE
FRANCE

My Dearest Savannah,

By the time you receive this, I suspect the trees in Montague Square will be pushing forth their first green tips, hesitant but determined. Here in the north of France, there is little sign of spring—only mud, endless mud, and that same grey sky which has followed us from Flanders to the chalk pits near Loos.

But something stirs. Not in nature, but in orders.

We are to move within days. The whisper has become a summons: Neuve Chapelle, they say. We will be the point of the spear.

The last week has been filled with sharpening. Of blades, of wits, of resolve. We've rehearsed charges in fields so pitted they resemble the face of the moon. We've memorised maps by candlelight, and traced roads with the tips of our fingers until they etched themselves into our minds. The officers are tense. The men quiet. I find myself strangely still.

There is a knowledge one gains only in war—not of glory, but of *intimacy*. I know now the way Bexley speaks when afraid (he jokes about poultry). I know the precise crack of Emery's rifle when fired from a prone position. Thompson, though brusque, kisses a photograph of his sisters before battle. I used to find him arrogant. I now see only love, hidden beneath grime and wool.

This war has made us more than comrades. It has made us *kin*. Not of blood, but of bond. I do not know if we shall all return from this next ordeal, but I do know that each man beside me would sooner die than let the other fall alone.

And I—I shall not fall. Not yet. Not while I still have letters from you pressed against my chest, and dreams of you standing beneath the gaslamps in London, waiting, smiling, daring me to be more than this.

Savannah, I must tell you something that presses in my mind like a second heartbeat.

The night before last, I awoke from a strange sleep. Not startled, but alert, as if summoned by something just outside the tent. I stepped into the dark and walked a few yards beyond the line, past Percy the goat (who grumbled at my presence), and stood beneath a leafless tree, alone.

There, I thought of the secret again—the one my father hinted toward, the one buried beneath the red barn in New York, under the floorboards and the roots of that oak tree, beneath the cornerstone of something not yet built. I imagined unearthing it with you. Not for treasure, not even for legacy, but for *belonging*. For knowing that he had seen this future in us, before we had.

And then I remembered his final words to me: *"Lead with steadiness, love with courage, and when the time comes—build."*

The word clanged in my heart like a railway bell. *Build.* Not merely survive.

I long to build with you, Savannah. A life. A place. A purpose greater than all this ruin.

If you were here now, you'd laugh at how sentimental I've become. "The war poet returns," you'd say. And you'd be right. But I do not apologise. In times like these, to feel deeply is to remain human.

I write you this knowing it may be my last before the assault. I do not say this to frighten you, only to be honest. We charge soon. Perhaps even by the time this reaches you, it will already be done.

Know that I am not afraid—not in the way I was before. I know my place, I know my men, and most of all, I know *why* I fight.

For England, yes.

For honour, certainly.

But for you, Savannah Langdon of Bristol, living in London, dancing in dreams and alive in my every breath—above all, I fight for you.

Ever your devoted,

Wesley A. Crosington
Acting Corporal, Royal Wiltshire Rifles
Commanding Officer, Crosington's Ghosts

March the 13th, 1915
Montague Square, London

My Most Precious Wesley,

The bells rang out from St. Martin-in-the-Fields this morning—clear and certain, in defiance of the grey. I had not intended to pass through Trafalgar, but I was drawn there, as though the city itself were whispering for me to listen. The pigeons rose and scattered as the bells struck eight, and the great lions remained unmoved, watching the world tilt ever further into the unknown.

Wesley, it has begun.

Not merely in papers or whispers—but truly. The war is no longer distant thunder. It is here. It has entered the marrow of our streets. The posters are everywhere—*Your King and Country Need You.* Men queue in the cold to enlist. Boys younger than my brother lie about their age and return home with shining eyes and new uniforms.

I am frightened. And proud. And torn.

William has written again. A single page, dated from Saint-Omer. He has been formally attached to the British Expeditionary Force—he calls them *The Old Contemptibles*, with a sort of reverent defiance. He said it was the Kaiser himself who gave them that name, and that it rather suits them: seasoned, sharp, and utterly unimpressed by tyranny.

He ended the note with: *"Tell Savannah not to fret—I've already won three games of chess and commandeered a moustache comb."*

Mother wept. Father nodded and left the room. I, as usual, went to the press and set type until my hands forgot how to shake.

I do not think William truly understands what lies ahead. But then, who among us ever does?

To distract myself, I've thrown my efforts fully into the war committees. Bethany and I chaired the St. George's Hospital Ball last Thursday at the Savoy, and what a glittering affair it was—music, dancing, and speeches from everyone from Lord Kitchener's secretary to a widowed Countess who insisted on toasting "the brave lads of Wiltshire," at which I nearly fainted.

Kimberly has joined the Ladies' Ambulance Corps as a "non-uniformed supporter," which I believe is a fine way of saying she has not yet passed her test in bandaging. She wrapped Bethany's thumb so tightly yesterday that it turned violet. We had to cut her free with a fish knife.

There are days, dear heart, when I do feel like a fraud. I sit in drawing rooms filled with violets and lace, eating puff pastry and discussing field hospitals I've never seen. Yet I persist. We all must do something.

In the quieter moments, I read your letters again and again. Yours from Neuve Chapelle shook me, more than I can say. I read it aloud to my mother and then folded it into a blue ribbon I've tied beside my mirror. Every morning, I look to it, and whisper: *Let him come back to me whole.*

There is a tree I pass in Hyde Park—a gnarled old sentinel, half-strangled by ivy. I think of the oak you described. The red barn. The cornerstone. And though I do not know what lies beneath it, I believe in its promise. In its whisper of a future untouched by war.

Come home to me, Wesley. When you can. However you can.

Until then, I remain your
Savannah Langdon
Daughter of ink and iron

London, 1915 – The Home Front Sharpens

By March, London had changed.

The first crisp air of spring did not bring the usual renewal, but rather a strange, suspended breath—as though the whole city awaited something immense and terrible.

Savannah Langdon stood at the centre of it all: the ink-stained daughter of a newspaper baron, a reluctant socialite turned wartime hostess. The war was no longer a curiosity—it was a devourer. And yet, she persisted.

She spent her mornings in the pressrooms, sleeves rolled, fingers black with type ink, assisting her father's operations with quiet authority. He still ran the Langdon papers, but more and more, he relied on Savannah's instincts. She knew which stories stirred courage, which headlines rallied the people, and which truths could be borne without breaking hearts.

Her afternoons were divided between charity balls and hospital meetings. She became a familiar figure at the War Office Ladies' Committee, working alongside society women who once only debated silk patterns. They now argued over rationing schedules and troop supply routes.

Bethany and Kimberly were her constant companions in these endeavours, providing both levity and loyalty.

Bethany had taken to quoting Edith Cavell, the British nurse executed by the Germans in Belgium, with a fervour that made society matrons slightly uncomfortable. Kimberly, ever theatrical, had begun dressing in dark navy and insisted on being addressed as "Nurse Kimberly of the Back Row Brigade."

Together, they found ways to laugh amidst the mourning.

One evening, after a particularly grim report came through from the Marne, the three girls snuck into the Langdon printing house after hours and printed a fake newspaper edition headlined: *"Goat Named Prime Minister; Percy Promises Peace by Tuesday."* They delivered it in envelopes to their neighbours. For a brief moment, laughter replaced fear.

But the undercurrent of dread remained. Savannah felt it most sharply in the letter from her brother.

She remembered the summer of 1903, by the River Avon, when William—Pepper, always Pepper—had constructed a trench using old apple crates and declared war on the trout. He wore a bucket for a helmet and conscripted Savannah as his intelligence officer, charging her with delivering pebbles (coded messages) to the "Eastern Front," which was actually the far side of the orchard.

Now, her brother was somewhere in France, holding a real rifle. The boy who once played soldier now *was* one.

She couldn't sleep that night.

Instead, she sat by the fire, wrapped in one of Wesley's old coats (smuggled home before his deployment), and read his latest letter again. The imagery of the barn—the oak tree, the stone, the buried secret—danced before her like a fairy tale. It comforted her more than she'd admit.

A future. A home. Something beyond this inferno.

That hope, fragile though it was, became her lantern in the dark.

And she would keep walking, keep writing, keep *believing*—until it guided them both home.

CHAPTER XI

MARCH THE 16TH, 1915
FIELD HOSPITAL, SOMEWHERE
NEAR NEUVE CHAPELLE
FRANCE

My Most Treasured Savannah,

I write to you with hands stiff from cold and stained with the dirt of a world gone mad. We are alive, though only just. The Ghosts held the line—and more. We broke through. For forty-eight hours, we surged across blood-slick fields and shell-pocked farm roads, through barbed wire and boiling lead, until we reached the smoking remnants of Neuve Chapelle itself. And then we held it.

I do not exaggerate when I say that I have seen the edge of this world.

We went over the top before dawn on the 10th. The bombardment that preceded us—my God, Savannah, it was thunder and fury incarnate. The very earth screamed.

98

For thirty-five minutes we fired every gun we had. The sky turned black. And then, the order came.

"Forward, lads. Walk smartly now."

And so we did.

You might imagine that the first few steps out of the trench would be the worst—but no. It was the tenth. The one where you realise you are truly in the open, and the mud grabs your boots like hands, and every breath feels borrowed.

Emery went down beside me at the eleventh. A piece of shrapnel caught his side. I saw him wince, press his hand to the wound, and continue walking. "It's not your fault, sir," he said, as though I had apologised. "I needed a rest anyway."

We reached the German front line faster than expected. Their wire had been shattered by our guns. But what awaited us behind it was not surrender. It was a second line, dug deep and filled with men who fought like wolves.

There, in the fog and fire, we fought with bayonet and boot. There was no grand charge. No elegance. Just grit and fury and the certainty that one must stand or all would fall.

At one point, I found myself back-to-back with Bexley in a crater the size of a stable. He had a revolver; I had a broken rifle and my father's penknife. He looked at me and said, "Well, Duke, looks like we're dancing."

We survived.

We retook Neuve Chapelle.

We held our position for three more days.

I will not lie to you—our losses were sharp. Emery, brave and unflinching, did not rise again after the second night. Thompson lost a leg but lives. Percy the goat, absurd as ever, was found chewing on a dispatch envelope in the ruins of a bakery. I have never been more grateful to see a beast I once swore to roast.

The men—what remains of them—are sleeping now. I sit outside the canvas of our medical tent, wrapped in a greatcoat several sizes too large, watching the sky turn to ash. My ears ring still. The world feels distant, as if I am writing to you from the other side of glass.

And yet I must write.

Because it is you who anchors me to the world we're meant to return to.

You, Savannah, and the vision of a house not yet built, under a sky not yet marred by artillery. A home beside that red barn. The one my father stood in once and said, *"This is where your future begins."* He buried something there—I know it. Something for us. A promise. A legacy.

I intend to find it. With you.

When this war is done—and it shall be done—we will go there. We will dig beneath the boards and the oak tree's shadow and find what he left for us. And we will build.

Not just a house. A life.

I write this with blood on my boots and earth in my teeth, but I write it with *hope*, Savannah. Hope more powerful than shells. Hope that no German steel can pierce.

I will sleep now, with your letter beneath my head. And I shall dream of you, waiting at the station, looking as you did on the night we first danced, eyes full of fire.

Yours always,
Wesley A. Crosington
Acting Corporal, Royal Wiltshire Rifles
Commander of Crosington's Ghosts

March the 20th, 1915
Montague Square, London

My Most Dear Wesley,

Your letter from Neuve Chapelle arrived yesterday. It took me three sittings to finish, not for lack of desire, but for the unbearable thrum in my chest each time I imagined you there—in that crater, shoulder to shoulder with Bexley, the roar of war crashing about you like waves over stone.

I trembled as I read it, yet I could not look away. You are no longer the man I watched kiss my glove beneath the elm tree at Kensington. You are something more—something forged.

When I read of Emery's passing, I wept. I did not know him, not truly, but your words brought him to life in our parlour, as real as Father's pipe smoke or Mother's piano etudes. I lit a candle for him at St. Mary-le-Bow. His name now sits beside your own in my daily prayers.

103

I will keep this brief, though my heart is anything but quiet. Your courage—no, your *constancy*—reminds me of the very England we seek to protect. Not the flags and titles, but the steadfastness of spirit.

Please, if Percy the goat survives this war, I demand you return him with you. He seems a fool, but he is a survivor. Like someone else I know.

Yours in devotion,
Savannah Langdon

London, March 1915

As the Battle of Neuve Chapelle was fought in the mud-churned fields of France, across the Channel, London's drawing rooms buzzed with their own kind of strategy. Not of bullets and bayonets—but of influence, wealth, and persuasion.

Savannah Langdon received Wesley's letter amidst the clatter of tea trays and newsprint. Her father, William "Bill" Langdon, had taken to reading war reports aloud at breakfast, peppering each grim dispatch with a grunt, a curse, or—in rare moments—a smile of admiration when word came of Wesley's leadership.

To Savannah's immense relief, Wesley's father, the formidable William Crosington, had improved markedly. What was once feared to be a mortal decline had, thanks to a brilliant physician from Oxford and sheer bull-headed refusal to die, turned around.

The elder Crosington, though frailer in body, remained iron in will. And he was now planning a voyage.

Together, William Crosington and Bill Langdon would sail to America—not for escape, but for purpose. Their mission was twofold: to raise funds for the British war effort and to court the influence of American powerbrokers. While the United States remained officially neutral, there were hearts and fortunes in New York that could yet be stirred.

And stirred they would be.

J.P. Morgan, the titan of finance, agreed to meet the men at his Murray Hill mansion in New York. A master of consolidation and transatlantic influence, Morgan had already begun extending credit lines to Britain through his firm. With the promise of rail expansion and newspaper syndication, he showed interest in more than just bullets—he saw *industry*.

Andrew Carnegie, long retired from steel but still a patron of great causes, offered his thoughts from his estate in Lenox. Though Scottish by birth, his love for Britain remained keen. In a private meeting with William Crosington, he expressed support for modernising the *Trans-Atlantic Exchange Corridor*—the envisioned bridge between British rail and American ports. "Railways win wars," he reportedly said. "And after war, they carry peace."

Meanwhile, John D. Rockefeller, enigmatic and cautious, opened his Palm House at Kykuit for tea with Bill Langdon. Though his support was less vocal, he pledged to expand ink and press delivery to American towns along the Hudson. In private, he admired the scale of Langdon's syndicates. "A clean press," he mused, "builds a clean people."

Back in London, Savannah tracked all of this by letter and telegram, her father's updates delivered between sips of tea and the scratching of type on the editorial floor.

She felt the gears of empire shift.

These were the foundations of a *future world*—one not yet built, but visible just beyond the veil of war.

Savannah often imagined Wesley, muddy and noble, standing in the red barn his father once visited in the Hudson Valley. That barn would one day become the cornerstone of the *Crosington Central Station*, the start of something magnificent.

Under that oak, beneath those floorboards, lay a gift—a secret meant for two hearts bound by war and destined for legacy.

And in London, Savannah dreamed of trains yet to run, presses yet to print, and the moment when, at last, she would see Wesley's silhouette emerge from the smoke and steam of a platform not built yet, but already alive in her heart.

CHAPTER XII

MARCH THE 28TH, 1915
NORTHERN FRANCE, BEHIND
THE FORWARD LINES

My Ever-Steady Savannah,

The war shifts, like weather on the moors—one moment grey and grinding, the next alight with something altogether new.

Today, that newness arrived in the form of a woman. Yes, my love—a woman, uniformed, sharp-eyed, and utterly immune to the boys' clumsy attempts at gallantry. She stepped out of the transport like she'd been walking through artillery smoke her whole life, and with one glance at the Ghosts, she assessed us all as if we were a row of mismatched books on a shelf.

Her name is Miss Albright, or rather, *Lieutenant Albright* of the British Military Intelligence Bureau. And yes, she is a proper officer. Apparently, Command has finally decided to make use of certain... underutilised assets in the field. Unofficially, she's here to "observe and relay tactical nuances to headquarters." Officially, she's with us until further notice.

Bexley, of course, has not stopped talking since.

"I always said this outfit needed a good brain," he told her upon introduction, grinning like a fox in a henhouse.

She raised an eyebrow. "Then it's a wonder you were permitted to remain."

He was silent for the first time in three years.

There's something curious there, Savannah. I cannot put my finger to it—nor should I. Military protocol is firm. Romances in theatre are strictly prohibited, and we Ghosts are not just any unit. But still... there was a moment at dusk. I caught them both smoking near the munitions tent, shoulders brushing in that way which pretends not to notice it's happening at all.

I said nothing.

We all need something to tether us. Even fools like Bexley.

Tomorrow, we move again—north, toward Arras. Rumours stir of a German artillery buildup there, and our orders are to infiltrate and disrupt. Lieutenant Albright claims to have access to trench maps the likes of which even Command haven't seen. "Drawn by a French spy with a death wish and a fountain pen," she said. I like her already.

The men grumble, but they go. The Ghosts are not what we once were—our numbers thinner, our eyes more tired—but what remains has tempered into something ironclad.

And through it all, I carry you with me.

I find your letters folded perfectly, always pressed like pressed violets between the pages of my field book. I read them under makeshift lanterns. I read them beside the fire. I read them when I fear I've lost myself to the smoke and noise.

And I dream of a place far from all this.

A patch of land in New York. You know the one. There, behind the red barn, beneath the oak, lies something my father placed long ago. I do not know what. He never told me. Only that one day, *when all was still*, I would return to it. I believe now, more than ever, that it is meant for *us*.

Let us endure, my darling.

Let us win this fight.

And then, let us dig and find what secret is burried—not for treasure, but for what endures.

Yours eternally,

Wesley A. Crosington

Captain (provisional), Royal Wiltshire Rifles

Commander of Crosington's Ghosts

April the 2nd, 1915
Montague Square, London

My Most Constant Wesley,

I confess your last letter left me pacing the corridor of Father's study for a full hour before I could reply. A woman in your ranks? I clutched the envelope and re-read the sentence as if my eyes had lied the first time.

And yet—my heart did not leap to jealousy, but rather to something stranger: *curiosity*. The kind of curiosity one feels when watching a chessboard rearranged before one's eyes. A woman at the front—*finally*, I might say. Lord knows we've been organising, fundraising, and nursing since the first shots were fired, and yet not once has the Army seen fit to send us where the true decisions are made.

You must tell me more of this *Lieutenant Albright*. From your description, I gather she suffers neither fools nor flattery. Good. Bexley could do with a dose of both.

Bethany and Kimberly have taken to inventing wild tales of her exploits. In their latest version, she is a

Hungarian countess-turned-spy who once seduced a Prussian colonel in order to steal his trench maps and escape in a stolen motorcycle. I daresay the two of them would make excellent novelists if they ever stopped drinking sherry in the mornings.

But I digress.

London grows more restless by the day. The wounded are returning in greater numbers, and the streets echo with ambulances and solemn footsteps. And yet, amidst the mourning, society carries on. Last week, I attended a fundraising gala at the Savoy—gold-laced invitations and all—to benefit the Red Cross transport corps. I wore blue silk, as you once admired, and gave a modest speech on behalf of the Langdon Press.

We raised over five thousand pounds.

It hardly feels enough. And still, I do what I can.

I long for your next letter, and for the sound of your voice in our garden once more.

Hold fast, my dearest. And if the mysterious Lieutenant Albright should offer a knowing smile to Bexley, do tell him from me that I expect a full account upon his return.

Yours in all storms,
Savannah Langdon

London, April 1915

In a time when telegrams carried grief as often as news, and newspaper boys shouted the word "casualties" more than any other, London persisted. It hummed, teetering between dread and duty.

Savannah Langdon had learned to live in the in-between.

With Wesley now weeks into a new campaign and the Ghosts marching toward Arras, her letters took on new weight. She re-read his words not once but thrice, memorising the cadence of each sentence, the turn of each phrase—each one a flickering candle in the drafty cathedral of war.

But life did not wait. Especially not at the Langdon Press.

With her father, Bill Langdon, now travelling often—either in France for reports or planning the great American venture with William Crosington—Savannah found herself stepping into a role she had long observed but never claimed.

On March 29th, she oversaw the printing of The London War Chronicle, a new weekly sheet intended for both the capital's intelligentsia and the families of enlisted men. It featured accounts from field correspondents, war poetry, and curated telegram reports—all fact-checked and tempered by Savannah herself.

She corrected typesetters, rejected a poem she found "entirely too French," and rewrote a column titled *"What To Send Our Boys"*, which originally suggested champagne and silk socks. Under her pen, it became a practical guide—woollens, dried tea, small brass crucifixes.

"Better than lace," she muttered, half to herself.

Meanwhile, the papers whispered of a "female operative" now embedded in British lines—rumours thin as smoke, but enough to ignite society's imagination. Some said she was Churchill's niece; others claimed she once killed a German spy with a parasol. Savannah knew the truth would be far less romantic—and far more interesting.

At the Montague Square house, Bethany and Kimberly kept the mood light.

On April 1st, they hosted what they called a *"Spirits and Strategies" Salon*, a strange hybrid of séance and social gathering, where one moment they toasted to the souls of the departed, and the next plotted an imaginary invasion of Berlin using maps from Father's encyclopaedia.

In quieter hours, Savannah walked alone to the embankment, her gloved hands clasped behind her back. She thought of Wesley. Of the parcel of land in New York. Of the red barn, and the secret beneath the oak tree. She wondered if the wind ever rustled the boards in his absence.

She did not know what lay beneath them. But she believed, more than ever, that it was meant for her.

For them.

And so she wrote, she led, and she waited.

Always waiting.

CHAPTER XIII

APRIL THE 8TH, 1915
NORTHERN FRANCE

My Dearest Savannah,

How strange it is that in a place surrounded by smoke, soot, and the incessant rhythm of war, my mind wanders so vividly to a day of sunshine and civility. Forgive me if this letter carries no reports of artillery placements or whispered strategy—today, I write to remember.

Do you recall that spring day in London? I should think you do, for it has etched itself into my soul as a painting might remain fixed upon a wall long after its painter has faded to dust. It was the last Thursday of March, the year before the war—1914, though it feels a century past.

You wore that pale lilac dress, the one with the tiny pearl buttons and the lace collar that fluttered slightly in the breeze. We met at Hyde Park, near the Serpentine, where the swans seemed to move as though aware they were performing for the more civilised class of spectator. I remember you laughing when a boy on a bicycle nearly ran headlong into a hedge and I, ever the gallant officer, offered only a subtle raise of my brow. You accused me of *delightful English arrogance.* I never denied it.

We strolled the Lady's Walk, arm in arm, speaking of politics, poetry, and the absurdities of society. Do you remember that old gentleman with the waxed moustache who stopped us and offered a dog biscuit to Percy the goat—who had insisted on following us from the stables? You managed it all with your usual charm, introducing him as *"Sir Percival of Wiltshire, honorary Duke of Chevre"* to the immense delight of the old man.

Later that evening, we were invited to the Spring Ball at the Royal Automobile Club, hosted by the ever-glorious Duchess of Marlborough. You were incandescent beneath the chandeliers. The room was awash with satin and spats, a glittering constellation of privilege and powdered cheeks. The band played a Strauss waltz, and I remember thinking as I led you to the floor that there could never be another woman who filled a room so wholly with grace.

We danced—Lord, how we danced. I fear I trod on your toes more than once, but you never flinched. You told me then, while brushing a wayward curl from your temple, that you believed I was "not long for mere parties," that I had "the air of someone made for destiny."

I thought it nonsense at the time.

But now, amid the quiet moments between chaos, I hear that phrase again. And it reminds me that the man I wish to be is the man I was on that ballroom floor—eyes fixed on you, spine straight, heartbeat sure.

The war may have tarnished my boots and tested my faith, but it has not dimmed the light I saw in you that night. In fact, it is that very light which sustains me.

I keep that dance tucked away in my memory like a pressed violet in a book of sermons—rarely opened, but always near. When the world is too loud, I close my eyes and I am once more beneath the crystal chandeliers, turning gently in time with you.

I will return to that life, Savannah.

And when I do, I hope there shall be another waltz—perhaps not as grand, perhaps only in our own parlour—but it shall be with you, and therefore perfect.

Always,

Wesley A. Crosington

April the 12th, 1915
Montague Square, London

My Heart's Keeper,

Your last letter reduced me to tears of the gentlest kind—the kind that fall without anguish but with such overflowing feeling that one dares not brush them away. How vivid your memory is, Wesley. How exact. I could see it all as if I were once again stepping out into Hyde Park, the scent of spring blossom in the air, your hand warm around mine.

I *do* remember the boy on the bicycle, and I remember laughing so hard my hat nearly flew from my head. I remember Percy the goat (how could I not?), trotting after us with more pride than a duke's spaniel. But what I recall most clearly, what never once faded from my mind, was the way you looked at me in the light of the ballroom.

You were in your deep blue coat—the one your sisters said made you look "unbearably parliamentary"—and I wore lavender silk, though I fretted over the hem for days. When you asked me to dance, I forgot every step I had ever learned. It didn't matter. The world faded, and there was only you.

I remember whispering, "Don't you dare step on me, Wesley," and you grinned and said, "Then stand still, and I'll simply turn the room around us."

Even now, that memory carries me through the greyest mornings.

The city has dimmed, my love. London is quieter at night, and even the gas lamps flicker like they are tired of burning. But your letter brought light into our drawing room again. I read it aloud to Bethany and Kimberly (well, most of it—some lines I kept just for me), and they immediately launched into schemes to recreate the ball in the parlour using tablecloths, sherry, and Father's gramophone.

The war feels nearer now. The newspapers whisper of fresh losses near Arras. I do not know exactly where you are, but I feel your presence whenever I stand in the garden at dusk. I tilt my face to the wind, and if it is from the east, I like to believe it brings something of you with it.

Thank you for the dance, even in memory.

And thank you for loving me still.

Forever,
Savannah

London, April 1915.

There are evenings when Savannah Langdon cannot speak. The world hushes itself around her—the servants tiptoe, the teacups rest untouched—and she sits at the window, a folded letter in her lap, her thoughts elsewhere.

Tonight is such a night.

Wesley's recollection of their promenade and the Spring Ball had stirred more than nostalgia—it awakened a part of her soul that had been in slumber. For though her days are filled with newsprint, charities, and coded telegrams from her father's travels, there are moments, rare and precious, where she is simply *the girl he danced with*.

The Royal Automobile Club's Spring Ball in March of 1914 had been a grand affair, marking the last season of peacetime splendour before the shadow of war fell. The Duchess of Marlborough had welcomed lords, MPs, journalists, and industrialists alike. That night, Savannah Langdon had danced with Wesley Crosington beneath shimmering chandeliers, while Percy the goat waited faithfully outside in the coat room (much to the scandal of the valet).

Savannah had known even then—long before he kissed her—that she loved him.

Back in the present, life demanded poise. The Langdon Press was operating under wartime strain. Ink deliveries were delayed, paper rationed, and half the staff now wore armbands from the Volunteer Corps. Bill Langdon, ever the storm-chaser, had departed with William Crosington to America to raise support for the war. Savannah received telegrams from New York and Boston, where her father spoke before financiers and industrialists.

She learned from one such wire that her father had met J.P. Morgan, who agreed to finance future expansions of Langdon publishing in exchange for exclusive access to war coverage. Morgan had also spoken favourably of a future investment in rail, and she knew that was meant for William Crosington's vision.

At a dinner in Manhattan, Andrew Carnegie had expressed excitement about forging new steel lines across the American landscape. "Wesley's family," her father wrote, "may soon have a transcontinental legacy."

John D. Rockefeller, always harder to pin, had offered instead to provide distribution networks for newspapers and supplies—his Standard Oil wagons reaching towns too small for post.

The future shimmered like distant city lights.

Back at Montague Square, Bethany and Kimberly had, true to their threat, recreated the Spring Ball. They wore borrowed silk gowns and danced through the hallway with exaggerated elegance, dragging Percy (still somehow alive and spirited) by a ribbon tied round his neck.

"We shall not be undone by a mere war!" Bethany declared, clinking her sherry to an empty candlestick.

"No, indeed!" Kimberly agreed. "A waltz a day keeps the Kaiser away."

Savannah laughed until she wept.

Later that evening, as she undressed by candlelight, she tucked Wesley's letter into her dressing table drawer. She did not lock it. She wanted it close, just in case she needed to hold it again in the middle of the night.

Because love, like war, required ammunition of the gentlest kind.

CHAPTER XIV

APRIL THE 17TH, 1915
NORTHERN FRANCE – NEAR THE BOIS DE LA FOLIE

My Most Beloved Savannah,

As I write this by the flickering breath of a stub of candle—tucked in a narrow trench no wider than a cart lane—I feel the sky cracking open above me with the dull rumble of distant shellfire. The morning air tastes of mud and steel. But still, I think only of you.

We were sent on a night mission last Sunday—my unit, Crosington's Ghosts, under the guidance of our new intelligence officer, Lieutenant Albright. The orders were to intercept and sabotage a telegraph line being laid by the enemy through a shattered grove known as Bois de la Folie—"The Madman's Wood," which is as welcoming as it sounds. I assure you, the name is no flourish.

Albright is—how shall I say it without offending your propriety?—an unflinching sort. Her face bears no trace of powder, her eyes are as sharp as a spring frost, and she speaks with the precision of a woman long used to being underestimated. I believe she may have once trained in Belgium, though she offers no personal details. Her accent holds the faintest trace of aristocracy, but she wears it like armour rather than ornament.

There is something curious between her and Bexley. At first, I thought it simple professional respect—he, with his dry wit and eagle eye; she, with her cool strategy and command. But now I begin to suspect something more delicate stirs beneath it. Last night, as we crouched behind a ruined stone wall near the enemy's signal post, she handed him a pair of field glasses. Their hands touched for but a moment, and though neither flinched nor blushed, a silence followed that was thick enough to slice with a bayonet.

I said nothing. One does not disturb what is still becoming.

The mission itself was perilous. We moved under a sliver moon, through blackened hedgerows and shattered stumps. The mud swallowed our boots nearly to the knee. Halfway to our objective, young Corporal Hensley—barely out of school, poor fellow—slipped into a collapsed foxhole and nearly vanished. Bexley hauled him out by the collar with one arm, muttering, "Good

Lord, lad, you can't be buried in France until you've first had a proper kiss."

We completed the sabotage. The wire was severed. Their communication disrupted.

On the return, enemy patrols passed within ten yards. We froze like statues of shadow. I held my breath so long I feared I'd gone to meet my Maker. But the patrol moved on, and we slipped back into the folds of the earth.

Lieutenant Albright offered a single nod of approval as we regrouped in silence. "Efficient," she said. "You ghosts do live up to your name."

I shall treasure that as high praise.

After we returned to our bivouac, and the men fell asleep one by one, I stayed awake to write to you. I often do. You are the last light I carry with me into sleep.

I thought then—strangely, amidst the ruin—that someday you and I might walk through a very different wood. One far across the sea, behind a property I have never named, but whose borders I know by heart. I can see it clearly: the old red barn, the oak tree, and the cornerstone beneath which lies something meant for you, and you alone.

We shall go together. I shall kneel beside you and lift the boards with my own hands.

Soon, my darling. Soon.

Ever Yours,
Wesley A. Crosington

April the 21st, 1915
Montague Square, London

My Dearest Wesley,

How odd it is that I now know the name of a place called *The Madman's Wood*, and that you have walked through it beneath a sliver of moonlight, unseen by the men who sought to end you. I read your letter beside the hearth, the light low, and I do not exaggerate when I say I held my breath with you—though I sat safe in a drawing room in London.

I dare not admit this to Father, but your account made me feel as though I stood with you among the shattered trees. Or perhaps I simply wish to stand there, if only to remind you that you are not alone in the shadows.

So, a woman is still among your Ghosts? I find this both thrilling and troubling in equal measure. You offer no name—only "Lieutenant Albright"—but I imagine her already. Tall, no doubt, and terribly clever. Kimberly insists she must wear rouge beneath her cap and carry a pistol in her stocking. Bethany thinks she's probably a widow and has a past. I told them both to hush and poured myself a second cup of tea.

But you speak of Bexley. Of hands that linger too long, of glances too quiet. I've always suspected he would be the first among you to fall to such things. It is perhaps his only flaw—that soft, loyal heart beneath all his sardonic grumbling. I do hope it does not end poorly.

The world here grows ever more involved. With Father and your dear Papa still in the Americas, the printing house has fallen under my careful, if mildly trembling, supervision. Do not raise your brows—I have not overstepped. I merely *observe with interest* and offer the occasional *strong suggestion* when the need arises. Mr. Pembroke, Father's long-trusted foreman, has been quite kind about my increasing presence, though he pretends to grumble whenever I inspect the galley proofs.

131

Our weekly editions now run leaner, with paper rationed and ink delayed due to a recent shipment stranded in Liverpool. Still, the presses thunder on, printing war bulletins, casualty lists, government appeals, and—most importantly—hope.

Your last letter, I read aloud to the compositors. When I reached the part about Percy, they laughed so hard that Pembroke dropped a tray of type and blamed it on "the ghost of Wellington." I've never seen hardened men so softened by a goat.

Wesley, you must not worry over the gift buried in America. I know you carry it like a sacred stone in your chest. I do not need to hold it in my hands to feel its weight. The knowledge that you think of our future at all—that you still imagine a field, an oak tree, a house—is the truest gift of all.

Keep safe. Keep writing. Keep remembering that there is a girl in London who reads your words until the candle gutters out, and then reads them again in the morning.

Forever yours,

Savannah

The Presses of War

In the bowels of Fleet Street, the heart of Britain's printed voice thundered on like a living engine.

Savannah Langdon had grown up with the scent of ink in her nostrils. It was the perfume of her childhood, mingling with coal smoke and the rustle of folded broadsheets. Her father, William "Bill" Langdon, had built his empire with type and timing—papers delivered before Parliament had spoken, stories inked before speeches ended. Now, with war tightening its grip, the presses had become weapons in their own right.

The Langdon Press operated three floors of machinery: two massive steam-driven rotary presses, each the size of a railway car, and four linotype machines, hulking brass beasts that clattered and groaned with every sentence composed. These linotypes—marvels of their time—allowed a single operator to set entire lines of type

133

in hot lead, replacing ten compositors with one trained man.

Or woman.

By 1915, with many of the male typesetters and pressmen conscripted, women had taken up the role. Savannah watched them work—sleeves rolled, brows furrowed—as they fed sheets into the guillotine cutter or adjusted the rollers on the galley press. They learned to listen to the rhythm of the machines. A misaligned gear, a late lever pull, and the entire sheet could be ruined. Time was ink. Ink was rationed. Every sheet mattered.

The pressroom was a symphony of noise—metal on metal, hissing steam, shouted corrections—and Savannah began to find music in it. There was Pembroke with his eternal scowl, Miss Davies on the proofing table with a blue pencil always behind her ear, and young George, barely fifteen, dashing between machines with messages and mugs of tea. These people weren't just printers; they were keepers of truth.

Each edition carried more than headlines. It carried morale. The stories of victory, of bravery, of survival in muddy trenches—those words lifted Londoners from dread. The photos, sent by telegram and printed in coarse half-tones, brought the war into every home, every café, every drawing room.

The Langdon Press became a lighthouse.

Savannah found herself drawn not only to the mechanical but to the editorial. She began reviewing columns, suggesting headlines, even daring to pen a short feature on the war effort at the Royal Hospital Chelsea. It ran unsigned, but Pembroke clapped her on the shoulder. "You've got your father's ink in your blood," he grunted.

Every evening, Savannah returned to Montague Square with soot on her gloves and new resolve in her chest. While the war tried to pull the world into shadow, she, too, was learning how to push back with light.

And when letters from Wesley arrived, she sometimes tucked them inside the editor's desk drawer—near the linotype instructions and paper ledgers. Because even in the house of ink and fire, it was *his* words that reminded her most what they were all fighting for.

CHAPTER XV

APRIL THE 29TH, 1915
FIELD HEADQUARTERS, SOMME VALLEY

My Most Treasured Savannah,

I hardly know how to begin this letter, for even as I write your name at the top of the page, I am reminded that my signature must now be signed Captain Wesley A. Crosington.

Yes, my love—*Captain.*

The promotion came without ceremony, as most things do in war. No brass band, no medals gleaming in candlelight, no proud toast in a London club. Only a mud-streaked envelope, handed to me at dusk by a courier whose boots squelched as he saluted. Inside it: a note from Command, a new badge of rank, and the directive that "Captain Crosington will henceforth take full leadership of reconnaissance operations for Sector 17-D."

And just like that, I became something more.

The men cheered when I read the orders aloud. Hensley leapt to his feet, Bexley whistled, and Dunne muttered, "'Bout bloody time." Someone found a bottle of plum brandy in an abandoned farmhouse, and we drank a victory toast out of enamel mugs, crouched around a fire no larger than a dinner plate. Even Lieutenant Albright offered a nod and the faintest glimmer of approval. (Which from her, I suspect, is tantamount to a standing ovation.)

Now, allow me to report a crime most grave, committed not by man, but beast.

Thistle, our noble goat and eternal nuisance, has stolen an entire loaf of bread from the supply cart. Not content to merely nibble it discreetly, she leapt up—graceful as a ballerina on hooves—and snatched it directly from the tin. Bexley gave chase, shouting curses fit for naval print. Thistle, for her part, dashed through the camp like a cannonball in a feathered bonnet, bread in mouth, until she finally settled on the roof of a dugout, chewing contentedly.

She is now something of a local legend.

The new men believe her a lucky spirit who cannot be killed. Hensley has begun composing odes to her in his notebook. Dunne made her a collar out of spent shell casings. Even Albright cracked a smile when she caught Thistle attempting to headbutt the camp's phonograph for playing too much Elgar.

I confess, her presence lightens the unbearable weight of days. As do you.

Tomorrow, we set out again. The Germans are fortifying a railway junction north of Bapaume. Intelligence believes they're preparing for a major move, one that could sever our lines. Our task: to infiltrate and sabotage the supply depot without being seen. Albright will join us. She and Bexley have grown close. Not scandalously—yet something sincere is forming there. I do not know if it will survive the war, but I pray it survives the night.

The world is a grim theatre just now, but amidst its ruins are small, defiant joys: a stolen loaf, a snort from a goat, a letter from you.

I think often of the land in New York. Of the barn and the oak tree. Of what lies beneath the cornerstone. Of a life not yet lived, but waiting, like a lantern unlit in the dark. We shall go there, Savannah. We shall walk the earth together and remember that the world was not made only for battles, but also for love, and laughter, and home.

Ever yours,
Captain Wesley A. Crosington

May the 3rd, 1915
Montague Square, London

My Dearest Wesley,

Captain! How it rolls from the tongue like music! How I wish I could have been there—no, not for medals or parades or to hear the rank announced, but simply to see the faces of your men when they heard the news. I imagine Hensley throwing his hat in the air and Thistle eating it whole. I read your letter three times before I could breathe properly, and then I held it to my heart and whispered "Captain Crosington" aloud, to no one at all.

Mother heard me from the drawing room and thought I had perhaps taken a chill.

I am proud, my love. But it is more than that. It is something deeper—like the sound of your voice threading itself through all the chaos of this world, steadying it.

Your tale of Thistle made me laugh so hard I nearly dropped my tea. Bread thievery! Goat acrobatics! I can see her now, perched like a queen atop a dugout, daring the world to interfere. I do believe she has more courage than most men.

As for Lieutenant Albright and Bexley... Oh, Wesley, I do not know whether to root for them or warn them. Love in wartime seems such a strange and splendid rebellion, like planting roses in a battlefield. Bethany thinks they must be writing secret poems to each other. Kimberly insists he has already proposed in code using the radio. I suspect the truth lies somewhere in between—quiet glances, perhaps, or the passing of a ration tin with just a touch too long upon the hand.

We London women grow ever more industrious. Just yesterday I spent six hours at the press reviewing a proof of the War Bulletin and then marched directly to the Ladies' War Relief Ball with ink on the underside of my wrist. No one said a word, but I caught Mrs.

Gainsborough eyeing me as though I might start setting type on the punch table.

The house feels quiet with Father still in America. Though I hear the occasional rumour that he and your dear father are shaking up all of Wall Street. I do hope they don't come back owning Pennsylvania.

I must away, as Summer is insisting I review her gown for Thursday's musicale. She is a dream and a storm rolled into one.

Yours in pride and longing,
Savannah

On Summer, the Curious Girl

Though Wesley Crosington marched through enemy territory with boots of mud and coat of dust, Savannah Langdon had begun navigating another kind of battlefield: the parlours and powder rooms of the London season.

And alongside her now, for the first time, stood her little sister—Summer Langdon.

Summer had recently turned seventeen, and with the war thinning the usual ranks of eligible gentlemen and giddy hostesses, she found herself pushed prematurely into the outer rim of society. But unlike many girls of her age who had spent years in preparation for presentation, Summer had spent hers in books, trees, and various emotional entanglements with orphaned animals.

"Your gown is fine," Savannah said gently as Summer spun before the mirror.

"It isn't fine, it's *predictable*," Summer pouted, tugging at the lace. "And Mrs. Hawthorne says I mustn't mention *bacteriology* during supper again."

"Why on earth were you talking about bacteriology at supper?"

"There was a questionable pâté."

Summer Langdon had a mind like a steel trap wrapped in silken ribbons. She spoke fluent French, passable Latin, and could argue with a Cambridge-bound boy about the finer points of translation from the Greek. Her favourite pastime was collecting discarded medical pamphlets from the alley behind St. Bartholomew's

Hospital and reading them beneath the apple tree in the garden.

She had, more than once, attempted to mend wounded birds with stolen bandages, or prescribe tinctures to her dolls for fictitious ailments. Once, scandalously, she had even stitched a torn coat sleeve belonging to their stableboy using a genuine surgical suture technique—learned from a book, of course. Savannah had found her in the kitchen afterward, cheeks flushed, muttering, "The incision was too shallow for proper testing."

And yet, despite this fierce intellect and drive, Summer remained caught in a world that would not have her as she was. Girls were to be presented, wedded, and wrapped into suitable silken forms—not sent to dissect cadavers or study internal anatomy. A Langdon woman as doctor? Unthinkable. Unpardonable.

Her beloved lady's maid, Elsie, had been with her since infancy, brushing her hair, hemming her stockings, and now—heartbreakingly—slowly being left behind. Summer had grown inches in months. She no longer needed help with corsets, nor to be reminded to read aloud from the Psalms. And it tore at her.

"I love her," she confessed to Savannah one evening. "But I'm outgrowing her, and I hate that. What if I never meet anyone who knows me better?"

"You will," Savannah said, though she herself had never known anyone better than Wesley.

Summer would debut quietly—no grand court presentation in wartime—and instead host an event of her own: a small soirée with Savannah, Bethany, and Kimberly helping arrange music, refreshments, and (if Summer had her way) a table full of microscopes for conversation starters.

"She wants to charm them with *paramecia*," Bethany whispered to Kimberly. "How delightful."

And so she read, and dreamed, and visited the wounded when permitted. She walked with a notebook tucked beneath her arm and spoke more to animals than men. But every day, she stood a little taller. The world might not yet be ready for Summer Langdon, but Savannah suspected the world had best prepare.

Because once the war was over, there would be women like Summer—clever, kind, and curious—who would no longer accept the corner chair in silence.

And perhaps one day, a Langdon daughter would wear a white coat and not a lace gown.

CHAPTER XVI

MAY THE 11TH, 1915
NORTHERN FRONT, SECTOR 17-D

My Beloved Savannah,

It is evening now, and the sky has turned the colour of ash mixed with rosewater. A strange peace lies over the camp tonight—not silence, for there is never true silence here—but something like stillness. The guns are distant, the crows have stopped circling, and even Thistle has curled herself under a canvas flap and ceased her usual torment of the supply wagons.

The men believe the lull is a bad omen. I believe it is simply the breath before the scream.

Tomorrow, we march eastward to recon a trench cluster near Miraumont. It's said to be recently fortified, heavily supplied, and crawling with enemy engineers. Command suspects they are building something. The phrase used was *mechanical advantage*. That phrase haunts me more than a full brigade of riflemen.

We have seen strange things, Savannah. The kind of things that make one question whether the old rules of war still apply.

There are rumours—confirmed only in fragments—of a new weapon, a kind of *armoured automobile*, fitted with caterpillar-like belts instead of wheels, capable of rolling over wire, mud, and men alike. They call it a "tank," though no one knows why. We have not yet seen one in the field, but a scout claimed to have glimpsed a hulking iron beast near Arras last week. He described it as moving "like a barn on whisky," loud as thunder, trailing smoke, with guns mounted on the sides.

Then there are the flamethrowers. Yes, my darling. *Flames.* Propelled from metal packs on a man's back, igniting the very air before him. The Germans have used them once or twice. The first time we saw one, we thought the devil himself had risen from the trench. The air stank of burnt linen and scorched earth. It is warfare transformed into spectacle—more terrifying than effective, but then again, terror is a kind of efficiency, is it not?

The machine guns are more familiar now, but no less dreadful. They chatter like demons at the slightest provocation. Whole fields can be cleared in seconds. I watched a flock of birds scatter over the no-man's land only to be shredded in midair by a single burst. I am ashamed to say I ducked—reflex, not logic. That moment stayed with me longer than any artillery barrage.

And the airplanes, my love! Oh, what a marvel. What lunacy. They are still rare enough that the men stop to point when one passes overhead, like children spotting a comet. The machines are nothing more than wooden skeletons wrapped in canvas and wire, their pilots dressed like bicyclists and armed with pistols or bricks. They fly not with confidence, but with faith—faith that the wind will hold, that the engine won't seize, that the wings, stitched with twine, won't peel away mid-spiral. One came down not far from us yesterday, a British scout—his engine sputtered, and he landed in a pond, cursing all the way down. When we helped pull him free, he offered us cigarettes and said cheerfully, "Well, that went better than last time."

This war, Savannah, is becoming industrial. No longer merely man against man, but steel against sinew, fire against flesh. It is a chessboard lined with gears and rivets, and we are but pieces made of blood.

And yet, in the middle of it all—there is still you. The sound of your name, the touch of your voice in memory, and the image of your hand, waiting for mine beneath that oak in New York. I do not care what machines they build. I do not fear any "tank" or flying carriage or infernal flame. Because none of them can undo what you and I are building. Quietly. Steadily. Across this war.

We found an abandoned gramophone today in a ruined church. The vinyl was cracked, but Bexley fiddled with it until it played a single, crackling verse of *Greensleeves*. The melody drifted across the trench like incense. Hensley wept and didn't hide it. I set my cap over my eyes and let the notes carry me to you.

Our little goat Thistle, you will be pleased to know, has taken to guarding my tent as though she were some great hound of the Highlands. She has chased off two thieving mules, one errant lieutenant, and an entire flock of chickens. She's very proud of herself. I believe she would lay down her life for my boots.

And me? I would lay down my life for a future where you and I may walk freely again through Hyde Park. Or through our orchard in New York. I know it is there—beneath the barn, under the oak, beside the cornerstone. I do not yet know what my father left for us. But I know it is *ours*. And we shall find it together, in peace.

Until then, I am your loyal Captain,

Wesley A. Crosington

May the 15th, 1915
Montague Square, London

My Dearest Captain,

I did not know that I could fall more in love with you than I already had. And yet, here I am—utterly undone, head over heels, all over again.

Your letter arrived while I was at the War Press, inking my gloves by accident as I tore the envelope open. I read your words in the corner by the linotype machine, forgetting entirely that the world around me was clanging and printing and shouting and bustling. It was just your voice, in my hands. Your voice, and your tales of iron monsters and brave fools with wings.

The way you write of the war's machinery—of tanks and fire-breathers and winged bicycles—it chilled me to the bone, and yet I could not stop reading. You paint them not merely as weapons, but as omens of the world to come. Still, it is your courage—your *steady courage*, Wesley—that holds me most in awe. You do not flinch. You observe. You command. And somehow, you write it all to me with such tenderness that I forget how much you are risking.

And Thistle! That goat is a national treasure. I've told Bethany and Kimberly that if ever the war should turn sour, we must petition the Crown to knight her. I have begun sketching a small badge for her collar: *Thistle, Guardian of the Captain's Boots*. She is as loyal and peculiar as her master.

I confess, part of me was tempted to place this letter inside the folds of a new pair of socks. You always forget how worn yours become out there in the mud. Perhaps I shall send them anyway.

I miss you terribly, but I am comforted—oddly, beautifully—by the thought of you listening to *Greensleeves* in the field. Somewhere between the rifles and the rivets, there you are, still finding music.

Forever yours,
Savannah

Of Ribbons, Romance, and Rising Spirits

As the machines of war grew louder on the Continent, London tried to hum its own tunes of civility and ceremony. In the Langdon household, that tune was currently a waltz of dressmakers, menu samplers, and invitation proofs. It was Summer Langdon's debut—or at least the shadow of one, given wartime's dampening of full court traditions—and Savannah was determined that her younger sister would be introduced with grace, joy, and just the right amount of mischief.

The planning had taken root on a Thursday afternoon, when the three girls gathered in the back parlour with parchment, tea, and far too many cherry scones.

"This mustn't be too fussy," Summer declared, waving off a sample invite with too much lace. "I don't want to spend my first party trapped beside a Viscount who only talks of pheasant."

"You could always request a Duke with no hobbies," Kimberly offered helpfully.

Bethany leaned over the tea tray, her long fingers brushing crumbs into her lap. "What about a scientific demonstration? You could open with a lecture on microbial fermentation."

"Now you're teasing me."

"Always," Bethany smiled.

Despite the laughter, each girl carried her own ache.

Bethany, ever composed and gentle, wore her grief in quiet sighs and small silences. Her fiancé, Greg, had been stationed with the Royal Army Medical Corps and was now overseeing logistics for field hospitals near Ypres. His letters came regularly, full of antiseptic smells and impossible delays, and he always included a poorly drawn rose in the corner, meant to represent Bethany's favourite garden at Montague Square.

"He writes that they've run out of chloroform and are using whisky again," Bethany shared one afternoon, folding the page delicately. "But he swears he won't operate after tasting it."

Kimberly, by contrast, sparkled through her uncertainty. Her "young man," as she called him (though she refused to name him directly), was a member of the Royal Naval Air Service, currently training in Scotland. Their courtship was playful, often conducted through scandalously short telegrams. Savannah once caught Kimberly scribbling a note on the back of a theatre program: *"You owe me a dance and a scandal. I'll collect both."*

"He says he dreams of crashing into me. Romantically," Kimberly confided. "I'm unsure if that's poetic or just alarming."

These contrasting loves—Bethany's steadfast, Kimberly's flirtatious, Savannah's aching and distant—wove themselves into the very fabric of Summer's preparations.

"I don't want a debut," Summer said one evening. "I want to *do* something. I want to be useful."

"You *are* useful," Savannah replied. "But the world isn't quite ready for a Langdon girl in the operating theatre."

Summer didn't argue. She only looked out the window, toward the streetlights flickering like stars, and muttered something about anaesthesia dosage.

And so they planned. There would be a *soirée*, but not just any. It would blend the elegance of the old world with the boldness of the new. Summer insisted on a small scientific exhibit in the corner—"for interest," she claimed—and a string quartet that would take requests, even for American ragtime.

The guest list included a smattering of sons of dukes, one girl with ambitions in journalism, two women from the nurses' corps, and the cousin of a pastry chef with diplomatic ties to Belgium.

"This," Kimberly whispered as she pinned a silk ribbon to Summer's dress, "will be a party they remember. Not for the gowns. For the girls."

And in that drawing room, for just a few moments, three women planned more than an event. They planned a future that refused to wait.

Next week, the invitations would be posted. The house would be trimmed with fresh ivy. And Summer Langdon, lover of books and baby squirrels and languages no one else in the room understood, would take her first step into society—with science, joy, and the full support of her magnificent, maddening, unforgettable friends.

CHAPTER XVII

MAY THE 27TH, 1915
FORWARD POST, VIMY WOOD, FRANCE

My Dearest Savannah,

I must write you now in a stillness I did not choose.

A dispatch arrived this morning bearing a seal I recognised too well. I knew before I broke it. My hands shook—not from fear of death, but from the deep ache of what I would find written within. The words were simple, nearly kind in their construction.

My father, William Crosington, has passed.

He died quietly, in his sleep, at the estate. There was no struggle, no pain. The physician reports his breath simply faded, as though he had exhaled the final worries of a long and burdened life. He was, they say, at peace.

I believe it. For I know he was a man who made peace with his Maker years ago, and with his legacy, I think, in more recent days. Perhaps that is why I did not feel panic—only a hollow echo, as though a great bell had rung somewhere deep inside me.

The men offered their condolences in the awkward, half-mumbled way soldiers do—Hensley patted my back with such force that Thistle nearly headbutted him in retaliation. Even Bexley, ever sarcastic, simply handed me his last dry cigarette and muttered, "For your old man."

It was all I needed.

The strange truth, my darling, is that I do not yet know what comes next. My father's holdings were vast, the steel empire complex, the railroad lines coiled like arteries across England and beyond. As his eldest son, many will now look to me—to govern, to lead, to shape what he built into something new. And yet... I am still here, boots in the mud, commanding a ragtag band of saboteurs and scouts who have taken to calling themselves *Crosington's Ghosts*. It seems almost a cruel trick of time that one might be both soldier and scion in the same breath.

And I must confess—though it shames me—I do not know if I am ready. Not for boardrooms, not for shares and ledgers, not for the burdens of commerce.

In my youth, I walked the yards with him—him with his hands behind his back, me mimicking his stride, both of us squinting at steel rails and axle widths. He always had a mind for logistics, for tonnage and turnarounds. I had a mind for maps and movement, but his? His was for systems. He knew how to move goods across an empire. He once said that running the railroad was like *conducting an orchestra where every instrument could explode.*

He and your father, Mr. William Langdon, were a force together. I still remember overhearing them laughing over shipping manifests and ink-stained crates. They moved newspapers and printing plates from city to city, ideas and ammunition in equal measure. They both believed in building things that mattered.

Their recent voyage to America was no small thing. Though my father had been somewhat frail before embarking, he insisted on going—saying a man must stand for his country before he lies down for rest. The sea journey was not kind to him, and I believe the Atlantic wind did little to strengthen his frame. Still, he carried himself with honour through each meeting, each appeal, each handshake. Upon returning to England, he attempted to recover, fighting as he always had—quietly, with discipline—but the exertion had taken its toll. The physician's report confirms what I suspected: the voyage hastened what time was already working upon.

And yet I cannot call it foolish. He believed in the cause. He believed in *you and me*. He went so that our children might know peace.

Do not think I am overcome, Savannah. I wept, yes. Not for the inheritance, but for the memories: the way he'd ruffle my hair as a boy when I solved a puzzle faster than expected; the proud nod he gave me the day I first wore uniform; the firm grip of his hand on mine before I left for France. He was never a man of many words, but when he said, "Make us proud," I knew he meant not just our family—but *our future*.

That is what I shall do.

There is no word yet from the War Office as to what they expect of me. I have not asked. I will finish this mission. I will not leave my men—*our men*—until I am ordered otherwise. They deserve more than a farewell in the night.

And if they do call me home, I know one thing: I will not return a boy seeking approval. I will return as a man ready to build. Whatever shape that takes, it shall include you, Savannah Langdon. We were always meant to build something together—whether it be a family, a future, or a station at the heart of the New World.

Do you remember that stretch of land in New York we spoke of—just past the orchard, near the old red barn? My father and I once walked there. I didn't realise it at the time, but he left something there. Something for us. I believe he hid it not as a riddle, but as a promise. I cannot say what it is yet, only that it waits beneath the oak, under the floorboards, beside the cornerstone.

And I shall not unearth it without you.

Yours, now and always,
Captain Wesley A. Crosington

June the 3rd, 1915
Langdon House, Belgravia, London

My Dearest Wesley,

I received your letter in the garden, where the roses are just now beginning their bloom, though I did not see them for quite some time after. The paper trembled in my hand as your words settled over me like a soft snowfall—quiet, steady, and impossibly heavy. My darling, I am so very sorry. My heart aches for you.

Your father was a great man. Not simply in title or legacy, but in spirit and bearing. To all who knew him, he was firm, fair, and forward-facing—never one to yield when something good could be built. I remember how his eyes would gleam when your name was mentioned in conversation. Even in his silence, he was proud of you.

And yes, I remember that voyage to America, when he and my father departed together in the name of industry and empire. It was brave, and it was costly. Papa told me once—after they had returned—that your father had insisted on standing for every meeting, even when seated would have been forgiven. He said William Crosington walked those corridors of steel and oil as though his soul had been forged in them. The voyage wore on him, I think. It was not the sea that weakened him, but the weight of what he knew must be done, and the urgency with which he gave himself to the task.

Papa has not spoken of it since.

I am glad he passed in peace. So few of us may choose the timing of our rest, and fewer still may take it at home, among things we love. Please tell me when the service shall be held. I will come, even if I must walk there myself.

Wesley—do not doubt your readiness. You were born for this. The steel is not only in the beams of your family's empire, but in you. It is in your jaw, in your kindness, in the way you think three steps ahead even when surrounded by mud and misery. Your father saw it. I see it. England will come to see it too.

Let the world look to you. And if they ask you to lead—whether in battle or in business—you will not do so alone.

Though your sisters are not permitted by law or station to hold such positions (and that is a cruelty I cannot abide), I do hope the right help finds you in the months to come. A man of vision must have trusted eyes at his side. And your sisters, I dare say, have the sharpest eyes of any in the realm.

Wesley, the thought of that land in New York has been often on my mind these days. I close my eyes and I see it—the hill, the barn, the low-hanging oak that catches the morning light just so. The idea that something waits for us there, something planted by your father... oh, it fills me with both dread and hope. Dread for the moment we must unearth it without him. Hope that whatever it is, it will be the first stone of the life we build *together*.

I carry you with me, Wesley. Always.

Yours faithfully and with deepest affection,
Savannah Langdon

June 1915 - Summers Ball

Though Savannah Langdon's heart ached for Wesley's loss, she did what so many women in wartime London had learned to do—she folded her grief neatly and tucked it away, not in denial, but in quiet deference to duty. In this case, the duty was her younger sister Summer's presentation to society—an event so long anticipated and so carefully arranged that it stood like a pearl on the Langdon family's timeline, unsullied even by sorrow.

The preparations had begun in earnest weeks earlier, but by the morning of the event, the house on Belgrave Square was transformed. Velvet ribbons and high white lilies adorned the entry hall, while the drawing room glowed with the warmth of beeswax candles and crystal sconces. A string quartet, brought in from Covent Garden, tuned gently in the background as footmen hurried in and out of the kitchen with polished silver trays.

Summer, now sixteen, had been fitted with a gown of soft lilac silk edged in pearl embroidery, her gloves the palest cream, and her shoes dyed to match. Her hair had been drawn up for the first time in the high Edwardian fashion—a modest tiara resting atop her curls, a gift from their aunt in Bristol.

As guests began to arrive, carriages lining the square like a parade of wealth, the rituals of the evening unfolded with an almost military precision:

First, the receiving line: Summer, flanked by her mother and elder sister, curtsied gracefully to each caller, her eyes wide but steady. Several older matrons murmured their approval. She was tall for her age, slender, with a brightness in her gaze that could not be taught.

Next came the supper, which had been arranged by the chef at Claridge's and brought in under heavy covers: cold poached salmon with cucumber aspic, quails' eggs on rye toast, veal in madeira cream, and a citrus syllabub so light it might have floated from the spoon. There were trifles and eclairs and champagne for the older guests, though Summer sipped politely from a glass of elderflower cordial.

Then came the true test: the first dance.

Tradition held that it be a waltz, and so it was—"Roses from the South," played with gentle swells by the quartet. Summer's first partner, a rather tall and angular boy named Lionel Percival Hughes of the Telegraphy Hugheses, led her with the awkward grace of a young man terrified of stepping on his companion. Still, they circled the floor with elegance.

But it was the presence of Benjamin Bradish, heir to the formidable Bradish banking dynasty, that caused the greatest stir. The Bradishes, though not titled, were among the wealthiest families in London finance, and Benjamin—broad-shouldered, clean-chinned, and educated at Eton—was considered a plum in the social orchard. His name appeared twice on Summer's dance card: once beside a polka (unusual for a debut), and again for the final quadrille.

This double appearance was no accident. According to Kimberly (who had made it her sacred mission to loiter near the punch bowl and gather whispers), Benjamin had asked to be introduced before the formal procession and had spoken to Summer at length about music, languages, and—curiously—horses. When Summer returned to the drawing room, there had been a blush in her cheeks and a brightness in her smile that not even Savannah had seen before.

Bethany, ever the motherly figure despite her own engagement to Greg (currently stationed in Rouen overseeing the allocation of surgical supplies), fussed over Summer's hem and posture, while Kimberly whispered commentary like a society page come to life.

"Did you see the way he looked at her during the quadrille?" Kimberly whispered. "He offered her his handkerchief! That's practically a proposal in Bradish circles!"

To which Bethany replied, "It's more likely he spilled champagne on his cuff and needed to hide it."

But even Savannah could not deny that something had stirred between Summer and Benjamin. A small flicker, perhaps, but one that might yet catch.

At the close of the evening, as the carriages were called and the guests departed with compliments and sighs, Summer stood by the window in her white gloves, looking out at the stars.

"Do you think I was terribly plain?" she asked.

Savannah shook her head. "No, my dear. You were radiant. You looked like you belonged there—not like someone who was presented to society, but someone who might one day lead it."

And with that, the house fell quiet, and the war beyond the parlour seemed, for a moment, a distant thing.

CHAPTER XVIII

JUNE THE 18TH, 1915
FIELD HEADQUARTERS, YPRES SALIENT

My Most Treasured Savannah,

There are days when the world turns so swiftly I scarcely know which way the sun rises. Since last I wrote, the soil beneath my feet has cracked and shifted—both here on the field and far away at home. I have much to tell you, and I ask your patience as I unravel it, thread by thread.

First, from home—my sisters have written.

Amiee-Elizabeth and Jennifer, my beloved and indomitable sisters, have seized the mantle of leadership at Crosington Rail and Steel. But not in name, for the world is not yet ready to see a woman's signature beneath the seal of empire. No, they shall govern in the shadows, beneath the polite and public face of Sir Roger of Dunnsburrough, Amiee's dear husband, who has offered his name for appearances only.

The very idea astonishes me. Jennifer, quiet and clever, now oversees freight contracts and locomotive repair orders. Amiee manages finance and personnel from a drawing room outfitted as a dispatch centre. Sir Roger, for his part, signs only what they place before him and nods nobly at meetings, offering an occasional "hear hear."

I am told that in only three fortnights, they've corrected a mismanaged shipment to Manchester, prevented a labour strike on the northern line, and negotiated a lower coal rate with the Welsh mines. All while attending luncheons and garden parties, so as not to arouse suspicion. Savannah, I am astonished. I am proud. I am in awe.

Though they cannot yet rule openly, they rule nonetheless—and it makes me wonder how many other empires are quietly stewarded by such capable hands. England's future may yet depend on its daughters, even if its laws do not yet recognise them.

Now, to war. And to something quite unexpected—someone, rather.

He arrived three days past.

Tall, lean, moustached in a way that suggests both humour and hardship. His gait is silent. His eyes—uncommonly alert. The papers call him *William Pepperday Langdon*. The lads call him *Sergeant Pepper*. And I—I remember him only vaguely, a boy of ten, once climbing apple trees in your father's garden.

He has been sent to us on loan—a special assignment, granted by the shadowed hands of military command. He is no ordinary soldier, Savannah. His record (what little I was permitted to read) glows with clandestine brilliance. Formerly of a deep-cover special operations unit, Sergeant Pepper has been embedded in operations across three fronts. He brings with him intelligence of the highest order, and training I have only read about in the faded scrolls of foreign martial disciplines.

Why is he here? Because we are preparing for something vast—an assault on a new and terrible enemy machine. I am not permitted to write of it in detail, but know this: it is real, and it is monstrous, and it must be stopped. Sergeant Pepper is here to help us do just that.

He is training the men under cloak of darkness—teaching us to strike silently, to move like shadows across blasted fields, and to survive what no soldier should be asked to face. He speaks of ancient tactics, passed down through obscure martial traditions: sudden, devastating strikes; movements made without sound; and the art of vanishing before the enemy knows one was there.

Already, the men follow his lead with wide eyes and sharp focus. Even Albright, ever skeptical of "foreign philosophies," now drills in silence each morning, moving like a wraith through fog.

Last night, Bexley and I brought Pepper into the officer tent for supper. He declined the scotch, accepted the sardines, and quietly redrew for us a German supply route from memory. When I asked how he knew such detail, he merely said, "I've been walking through their kitchens."

It is a strange thing, Savannah, to go to war with the brother of the woman you love. I suppose it shall either endear me to him—or make our dinners rather awkward once this is all over. But already I see in him something I trust. He is the sort of man one would follow into a hurricane.

As for lighter things, my dear Savannah: our goat, Thistle, has once again chewed through an ammunition map. I suspect she's working for the enemy—or perhaps she simply despises the science of cartography. Either way, she's been banished from the command tent and has taken up residence in Miss Albright's bedroll, which suits us well enough, as she's been called back to headquarters on some top-secret matter—or so she claims.

Bexley took her departure more quietly than I expected. He stood in the doorway of the mess, watching her go, saying nothing. Later, when I asked after his mood, he smiled faintly and admitted he'd never even learned her first name—and that somehow made her absence the more cruel.

There are few things sadder, I think, than unspoken beginnings—those fragile chances that slip away before one dares to give them a name.

The air grows warmer. The men's faces wear the dirt like old friends. We march again soon, and though the horizon holds only thunderclouds, I find myself steadied by strange hope.

Hope that my sisters shall rise.

Hope that Sergeant Pepper will lead us through the storm.

And most of all—hope for the day I return to England and you.

Write me of the lilacs in your garden.

Write me of laughter.

Write me of anything that is not this mud.

Ever and always,
Wesley A. Crosington

June 27th, 1915
Langdon House, Belgravia Square, London

My Dearest Wesley,

You must know I wept when your last letter arrived. I carried it into the garden, sat beneath the wisteria, and read it over and over until the ink blurred. Not from rain, but from the welling of my own eyes.

That William—your father, noble and full of devotion—has passed into glory, breaks my heart as if he were my own. He was ever so kind to me, even in my earliest visits to the Crosington estate, when I barely knew how to hold a tea cup without shivering. He once told me, when I had dropped my biscuit on the floor, that "true class lies not in never stumbling, but in knowing how to recover with a joke." I have never forgotten that.

It was no surprise to learn that he insisted on joining Father on that voyage to America, despite his frailty. You Crosingtons do not yield easily. I am certain that crossing was harsh on his health, but I find comfort in knowing he spent his final months *doing what mattered*, rallying men of influence for the defence of liberty.

And now you stand not only as his son, but as his legacy.

To hear of Amiee-Elizabeth and Jennifer—how marvelously they rise! My entire soul cheered when I read of their triumph. They are living proof of what the world too often refuses to see: that women are as capable of commanding empires as they are of hosting dinners. And Sir Roger, bless him, playing the perfect puppet to their invisible strings.

You must tell them, from me, that they are heroes. Not of the battlefield, but of the boardroom—and I hold their courage in the highest esteem.

And then, as if the world wished to lift my spirits higher still—you wrote of *William Pepperday Langdon*. My brother. Our Pepper.

You must forgive the childhood nickname—it persists. I could scarce believe my eyes when I read your description of him. Gone is the boy who carved swords from pine branches and declared battle on every daffodil in the garden. And yet... he is still *him*, is he not?

I feel proud and frightened all at once, knowing he stands now beside you, in such peril. But if he must be in harm's way, there is no man I would trust more than you to stand with him. Take care of him, Wesley. Please. He is my only brother, and your future best man—he simply doesn't know it yet.

As for London, the days grow long and heavy. The roses are blooming with abandon, but there's a hush in the air, as if the city is holding its breath. We attend fundraisers weekly—Bethany, Kimberly, and I. We wear cheerful gowns and dance with earnest young men who will soon ship off to war, their eyes full of dreams and dread. It feels both necessary and cruel.

I must close for now, as Summer is ringing the bell with excitement over a letter she has received. I suspect it concerns a certain banker's son—but I shan't ruin the surprise. More on that in my next.

Until we meet again—under trees, beneath stars, or at the gates of victory—I remain ever and always yours,

Savannah Langdon

London Society, Late June 1915

Savannah folded her letter with care, sealing it with the soft green wax she now reserved only for Wesley. She sat for a moment by the open window, listening to the low rumble of carriages and the distant clink of iron on stone. London—her London—was changing.

But change was not all sorrow.

Summer Langdon had blossomed. Since her radiant success at her coming out soirée, she had been the subject of many a drawing room whisper and ballroom murmur. And now, the first of what might prove to be many suitors had stepped forward—Mr. Benjamin Bradish, eldest son of the prestigious Bradish Banking House. His letter, sent in crisp penmanship on imported vellum, requested permission to promenade with Summer through Kensington Gardens the following Sunday.

It was all anyone could speak of.

Bethany, ever the romantic, had squealed when the letter arrived. Kimberly, her eyes alight with mischief, had insisted on designing Summer's ensemble for the occasion, declaring that "if the promenade failed to end in roses, it would not be for lack of millinery." Even Savannah's mother, usually distant on matters of courtship, had paused during embroidery to say, "The Bradishes are respectable. Very respectable indeed."

Summer herself had handled the entire affair with poise and grace, although a small smile betrayed her inward thrill. After all, she had always been the baby—tucked in libraries, whispering to rescued fox kits, scribbling Latin beside the hearth. Now she stood on the precipice of womanhood.

Yet even as her social debut bloomed, Summer wrestled with her own dreams. Her fascination with medicine deepened. She could often be found questioning the family physician about anatomy, or sneaking away with thick volumes on surgical techniques. Once, she confessed to Savannah that she wished to study the "invisible mechanics of healing," though she knew full well society forbade such things for women.

Meanwhile, back at Langdon Press, the machines turned day and night.

With her father William Langdon still abroad and entangled in matters of war funding and American influence, Savannah had taken more initiative in daily operations. The presses had adopted wartime themes—patriotic poems, illustrated children's books to raise morale, and informative pamphlets about rationing and home defence.

The printing floor—once the sole domain of men in rolled shirtsleeves—now welcomed a handful of determined young women, eager to support the effort. The machinery roared with life: belt-fed steam presses clanking in rhythm, linotype operators casting lines of metal type with speed and precision, and hand-fed platen presses churning out broadsheets by the hundreds. The smell of ink hung in the air like perfume.

Society, too, had changed its tempo. Afternoon teas were shorter, military updates replaced gossip, and newspaper headlines shaped conversation more than fashion did. Yet within this shifting world, Savannah and her circle kept joy alive. Their laughter echoed through the halls of Langdon House, even as distant gunfire echoed through the hearts of those they loved.

The dance of duty and desire had begun.

CHAPTER XIX

JULY 14TH, 1915
FIELD POST, NORTHERN FRANCE

My Dearest Savannah,

As I sit to write, the moon hangs like a polished coin in the sky, and the men rest in varying states of repose—boots off, letters tucked in breast pockets, soft murmurs passed beneath breath. Thistle, the goat (who surely shall one day have a knighthood of her own), has absconded again with a satchel of tobacco and is currently being chased by two corporals and a cook.

There is calm tonight. But it is the sort of calm that precedes something vast.

You see, Savannah—we now prepare for a strike. Not just any sortie or trench-advance, but a targeted operation meant to cripple the enemy's hold on the *Hindenburg Line*, that great cursed fortress they've dug across France like a scar. Our orders are clear: we are to infiltrate a supply depot believed to be a lynchpin for the line's northern support, just outside the town of Cambrai.

It is a warren of munitions tunnels and intelligence dispatches, camouflaged expertly, surrounded by sentries and wire, but—thanks to the intel delivered by a certain Sergeant William Pepperday Langdon—we know it is also vulnerable.

Your brother has become something of a legend among us already. The men call him "Sergeant Pepper," half in jest, half in awe, and wholly with respect. He has brought with him not only knowledge, but discipline. We move now under cover of night with an eerie quiet—no more clanging kits or whispered curses. We have become shadows.

He has taken to training us in what he calls *disruption tactics*—strike, vanish, mislead. We scale walls and crawl beneath barbed edges, mark escape points, rehearse demolitions, learn the cadence of German footfalls. It is a kind of warfare we've never known, and he—well, he learned it in the dark, in those hidden corners of the world no maps ever mark.

What lies ahead may shift the course of this war. The depot at Cambrai supplies not only shells and shot, but petrol, communications, and reportedly, experimental artillery not yet deployed to the front. If we succeed in destroying it, the Hindenburg Line may fracture.

And *if* it fractures, the enemy may finally fall back. The Ghosts may help crack the line that has stalled the whole of Europe for nearly a year.

Savannah—I write you this not to boast, but to steady myself. This is the most dangerous operation we've yet attempted. And it may well be the most important.

I think often of what we fight for. Not glory, nor medals, nor revenge. But for the right to return. To peace. To books half-read, and breakfasts not shared with lice, and gardens where one may sit beneath lavender without listening for shellfire.

To you.

There is talk that I may be recognised for leadership—though I think the real honour belongs to the men. They are brave, and clever, and full of impossible jokes. Bexley has begun keeping a tally of who can sneak closest to the goat without being headbutted (current record: three inches, held by Horace). And yet, in the next breath, they turn and rehearse a breach manoeuvre with the precision of dancers.

They are my brothers.

And Sergeant Pepper—your brother—is among them. You may rest easy in knowing that he is admired, well-regarded, and deeply respected. He does not seek attention. He earns it. We speak little of home, but I did once mention that I'd heard he built tiny ships from acorns as a boy. He denied it, of course. But he carved a mast from firewood that night and left it at my bedside.

Should this mission succeed, the war may yet shift. And I may yet find myself on the path homeward.

Until then, know this: the future we dream of together is more than hope. It is *reason*. It is *purpose*. And when we are through with Cambrai, I shall be one step closer to returning to you—whole, if not unchanged.

I remain yours,

Captain Wesley Anderson Crosington
Commander of Crosington's Ghosts
War Office Special Detachment: Cambrai Operation

London, July 20th, 1915
Langdon House, Kensington

My Dearest Wesley,

What a thrill it is to hear your words again, even penned across great distances, and to know that you are fighting not just as a soldier but as the guiding hand of something truly extraordinary. Your letters come like summer wind through open windows—brimming with life and breath, and yes, the scent of that ever-mischievous goat, Thistle.

The very notion of the Ghosts preparing to strike at Cambrai—a name already whispered in government drawing rooms—has sent my heart racing. Though of course the particulars are cloaked in secrecy, rumour and worry travel quickly here, and I now realise, with a strange clarity, that you are not only my Wesley but a thread in the grand weave of history itself.

And then there is William—my darling brother. I am astounded by what you've written of him. I always knew he had in him the makings of something noble, though I'll admit I had no idea the boy who once staged battles in

186

our mother's rose garden would one day lead true soldiers into darkness. When he wrote me last, he was characteristically vague, but there was warmth in his words—an unspoken bond forming between the two of you, I think. It comforts me more than I can say.

Things here in London are both lively and unnerving. The air is thick with a strange mix of celebration and sorrow. Bethany remarked yesterday that it is as though we are attending a ball in the middle of a storm, and no one wishes to acknowledge the thunderclaps at the door.

Speaking of which, I must tell you of an event most curious. I attended a garden fête at Lady Collingtree's estate—a "Patriotic Exhibition" they called it—with elaborate displays of wartime support, music, and even mock trenches assembled for the viewing pleasure of the aristocracy. It was both grand and utterly absurd. I cannot tell whether I was more amused or offended.

Bethany insisted on sneaking behind the bandstand to swipe two little Union Jack flags and proceeded to duel with Kimberly using them like fencing foils. They're truly incorrigible. The duel was interrupted only by the appearance of a horrified clergyman who mistook it for actual treason. I have not laughed so hard in weeks.

Summer, for her part, is blooming like a rose. She received a most proper note from Benjamin Bradish this morning requesting permission to promenade through Hyde Park this Sunday. She tried to act disinterested, but I saw how her cheeks coloured when she read the letter. I've offered to loan her my ivory gloves—though she insists her own lace pair are *perfectly sufficient, thank you.* She's quite serious about doing everything the proper way.

I must confess, I catch myself watching her with envy at times. The world still seems simple to her, full of gardens and poetry and dances by gaslight. And yet—there is something fierce beneath it. I believe she knows more than she lets on.

The presses continue to thunder at the Langdon house. The smell of ink, the weight of paper, the ceaseless movement of the typesetters—these things have become the rhythm of my days. I hope, in some small way, the truth we print finds its way into the hearts of men and not just the minds of them.

But for now, I sit here by candlelight, your letter in my lap, wondering how you looked when you wrote it. Were your boots muddy? Was your hand trembling from cold, or from memory? I imagine your brow furrowed with thought—and then, perhaps, that boyish smile you try to hide when Thistle does something scandalous.

Come home to me, Wesley. When the depot falls, when the Ghosts return, when this cruel storm has passed—we shall find our quiet again.

Ever yours,
Savannah Langdon

London, Summer 1915

Though war bled across the maps of Europe, London in 1915 moved with its own conflicted rhythm. The Langdon household, situated in genteel Kensington, found itself caught between two worlds—the high society of garden parties and patriotic concerts, and the dread that came with every telegram or tolling bell.

Savannah, radiant as ever, had taken to walking the corridors of her father's newspaper offices in her spare hours. The scent of ink was near-constant—heady, metallic—and the churning of the presses below echoed through the floorboards like a mechanical heartbeat. The *Langdon Daily Press* was booming. Demand for news—true or sensational—had skyrocketed. Every headline mattered. Every photograph was a spark.

Typesetters worked with extraordinary speed, their fingers blackened with lead and sweat, speaking in shorthand as if in battle themselves. Savannah took interest in every corner of the business, often pausing to ask the workers about their families or to read the test sheets before they went to print. One evening, she corrected a spelling error on the front page before the run began, impressing even the crustiest editor, Mr. Wexley, who begrudgingly admitted, "She's got her father's sharp eyes, that one."

Meanwhile, Summer Langdon's social debut, though just weeks past, was still the darling topic of Kensington conversation. Invitations to call upon her arrived in neat bundles. But it was Benjamin Bradish—the son of a respected banking family—who had caused the greatest stir. His request to promenade in Hyde Park was no minor affair. Savannah and her friends Kimberly and Bethany had spent hours debating its implications over tea and sponge cake.

Bethany, ever mischievous, wagered a guinea that Benjamin would propose before autumn. Kimberly, who still refused to be pinned down by any one gentleman, declared she would "bet double that Summer would say *no* just to stay mysterious."

The ladies also attended a rather curious high-society event in support of the war: the Patriotic Exhibition at Lady Collingtree's estate. Amid silk parasols and champagne, guests wandered mock-up trenches and were encouraged to "adopt a soldier" by knitting socks or writing letters. It was the oddest blend of frivolity and mourning. But such was life in wartime London—a dance balanced delicately on the edge of shadow.

Savannah, despite the heaviness in her heart, carried herself with poise. When she thought of Wesley—of his letters, of his men, of her brother in that same camp—she reminded herself that their love, and their cause, were worth the waiting. And as she watched Summer blush in response to Benjamin's latest letter, she dared to imagine that joy, like daffodils in the dark, would still bloom after the storm.

CHAPTER XX

AUGUST 2ND, 1915

NEAR CAMBRAI, FRANCE

My Most Beloved Savannah,

The night has become our companion—our cloak, our curtain, our confidant. We have begun our slow and deliberate crawl toward the heart of the enemy's supply line. This letter, though penned in haste and near silence, must reach you before the storm breaks.

The target is confirmed: a sprawling German depot tucked beneath the tree line just east of Cambrai. It is rumoured to hold munitions, gas shells, and a communication node—all vital arteries in the enemy's war machine. If we strike with precision, we may sever it entirely. The risk is immense, the reward greater still.

To this end, our unit has been bolstered once more by a rather familiar face.

Miss Albright has returned—reassigned from the War Office's covert intelligence division to accompany our latest operation. I was stunned when she stepped from the lorry three nights ago, her greatcoat drawn tightly at the waist, eyes sharp beneath her helmet, and that same unflinching calm I remembered. A woman on the battlefield remains a rarity, yet she carries herself as though she were born to command it.

Her orders were signed by a hand far above mine, and she brings with her the same air of secrecy she left us with—encrypted maps, cipher patterns, tactical blueprints, and the unspoken assurance that what she knows may alter the course of our campaign. The men were glad to see her again, though none more than Bexley. He tried to disguise his relief behind military decorum, but I saw the truth in the way his hand lingered at his cap when she passed.

What he does not yet know—what none of them know—is her first name. To them she remains simply "Miss Albright," the enigma in uniform who can read a cipher faster than most men can find their rifles. I suspect she prefers it that way; mystery is her surest armour.

Their reunion was brief—professional, on the surface—but there is a warmth between them now that wasn't there before she left. Whatever words went unsaid then seem to have found their courage in the interval. She keeps her field notebook close, and he keeps his uniform suspiciously immaculate.

You will laugh, my darling, but even Thistle—our obstinate goat—has resumed his old loyalties. He follows Miss Albright about like a footman and last evening tried to climb into her tent. She bribed him away with a biscuit and muttered something about preferring cavalry.

Your brother, *Sergeant Pepper*, has taken on the mantle of our shadow. He leads the night movements with the silence of fog and the cunning of foxes. We move in units of four now, breathing as one, crawling through the damp hollows of shell-cratered fields and rusted fences. His training is transforming the Ghosts into something closer to myth. Last night, we passed within twenty yards of a German patrol—no shots fired, no alarms raised. We were not men, Savannah. We were wind.

Despite the grimness of our task, there is camaraderie in this hell. Bexley and Godfrey argue over the merit of tea versus chocolate as rations. Wilkins now claims he's writing a novel. I suspect the only words he's penned are on the privy wall, but we let him dream. And I—well, I find solace in your letters, which I read each night before sleep, folded into the lining of my coat.

We strike within the week. The depot must fall.

And should we succeed, it may shift the tide. I do not know if I shall return from this operation, but know this, Savannah Langdon: my every breath, every step through mud and barbed wire, is for the hope of holding you again. There is no distance too great, no night too long, that would dim the fire I carry for you.

Until that glorious day, I remain—

Yours in light and in shadow,
Wesley

August 9th, 1915
Langdon House, London

My Dearest Wesley,

Your last letter sits upon my dressing table, worn soft from the number of times I have read it. I trace the edges each morning as though by some miracle it might carry me to you. I read your words aloud in the hush of night when all the house sleeps. I imagine your voice saying them—steady, warm, somehow invincible.

To hear of your mission and the silent movements through the French countryside fills me with both dread and admiration. Your description of Sergeant Pepper's methods—so quiet, so precise—sounds like something from a tale, and yet I know it is all too real. I am immensely proud of you all. I confess it is odd imagining Pepper as the midnight commander you describe; to me, he is still the little boy who once declared war on the frogs in the river near our grandfather's orchard. He fashioned a flag from a cravat and paraded about with his wooden sword, claiming the entire eastern bank in my honour. You will not be surprised to learn he kept detailed war maps then, as he likely does now.

I was most intrigued by your mention of the intelligence officer—Miss Albright—returned to your ranks once more. How extraordinary that she should be entrusted with so vital a task, and how glad I am that you and the men have her steady hand among you again. It takes a rare courage to face both secrecy and peril with such composure.

I confess I smiled at the thought of Bexley seeing her again; from your letters, I suspected there was a quiet fondness between them, the sort that words seldom dare to name. Perhaps her return will lend him some small measure of happiness in that desolate world of yours.

As for Thistle, I hope he behaves himself. The goat's loyalties are mercurial, but I cannot fault his taste.

Here in London, the summer blooms are starting to surrender to the crispness of autumn. We hosted a garden tea for the Red Cross ladies yesterday. Lady Ashcroft's hedges were trimmed into the shape of doves—though one appeared more like a wounded duck. Kimberly and Bethany were in high spirits, dressed in nearly matching muslin gowns and hats so wide they could shade a cart horse. The talk, of course, turned quickly to the war and to the latest dispatches.

Bethany, ever the mischievous one, whispered to me that she believed Bexley had fallen for someone in your unit. Kimberly all but squealed. I laughed, of course, and defended his good sense—but you must tell me if there's truth in it! You know how we live for such things while the world seems to teeter on the edge.

Summer, sweet Summer, is glowing from her recent promenade in Hyde Park with Benjamin Bradish. Mama and I observed from a distance (purely by coincidence, of course). He carried himself with a seriousness befitting a future banker, but the way he bent to listen to her—twice, no less!—told us he may be quite smitten. I am delighted for her. There is something unspoiled in their young attachment, untouched by the weight of war or worry. She wore the pale blue sash I embroidered with forget-me-nots, and I daresay it brought out a light in her that Benjamin could not have missed.

Wesley, I dream often of your return. Sometimes you are in uniform, sometimes not. Sometimes you are smiling, sometimes weary. But always—always—you are coming toward me. I wake before you reach my arms, but even so, it carries me through the day. Hold fast. You are not alone. All of London holds its breath for men like you.

With all my heart,
Savannah Langdon

August 1915

Though the winds of war reached every corner of England, London's high society continued to keep its rituals intact—perhaps as a way to maintain a sense of control over the chaos abroad. For Savannah Langdon, the war was an ever-present shadow, but one that did not fully eclipse the joys and dramas of daily life.

The Langdon estate, perched just beyond Kensington's edges, was abuzz with preparations. Summer Langdon's promenade with Benjamin Bradish had set tongues wagging from Knightsbridge to Belgravia. Benjamin, son of the formidable Lord Bradish—whose banking house handled much of the War Office's debt issuance—was not merely eligible. He was considered a golden ticket to both status and financial stability. But for Savannah, it was Summer's natural joy that mattered most. The younger Langdon sister had blushed furiously when Benjamin's name appeared on her dance card at Lady Wetherford's musicale. And again at the Ashworth garden luncheon, he had sought her out before even greeting the hostess.

Kimberly and Bethany were tireless in their commentary. Kimberly, in particular, thrived on the romance of it all. Her own flirtation with a junior officer had cooled (the poor man had been reassigned to Belfast), but she vowed to begin again—perhaps with one of the Bradish cousins. Bethany, ever loyal to Greg (now serving as a medical overseer in the Belgian corridor), was more cautious in her excitement, but nevertheless confessed to Savannah that she hoped Summer would not be "snatched up too quickly."

In the drawing room of Langdon House, the three women plotted Summer's future as though it were a chessboard. Dresses were discussed. Invitations speculated upon. Savannah, who was usually the most composed, surprised even herself by suggesting a September gathering with an open-air orchestra and honeyed tarts from Fortnum's. It would be the last event before the leaves turned, and possibly the last before letters like Wesley's became rarer still.

Beyond the parlor, the printing business continued apace. Savannah's father, Bill Langdon, now worked closely with partners in New York to expand their publishing reach. With the wartime need for updates, morale pamphlets, and official bulletins, demand for high-speed printing presses had never been greater. Savannah often visited the family's Fleet Street facilities, where the clang of the Linotype and the scent of fresh ink grounded her in purpose. The workers—many of them women now—were swift and tireless, their fingers blackened with type grease and resolve.

And yet, in the quiet hours, Savannah still walked the corridor outside the old nursery, tracing her fingers along the frame of a map Wesley had drawn years ago—routes of fictional railroads and shipping lines that had stretched across oceans and dreams.

She did not weep often. But when she did, it was for the space between letters.

CHAPTER XXI

AUGUST 15TH, 1915
SOMEWHERE IN NORTHERN
FRANCE

My Beloved Savannah,

I write to you by lantern-light, nestled in the hushed belly of the woods, where the damp earth muffles our movement and the stars above blink with knowing silence. It is the calm before something fierce. The air is thick with tension—like the breath held in a chapel before vows are spoken. Our mission draws near, and though I cannot share all its intricacies, know this: what we attempt may shift the tide.

Your last letter was balm and flame both. You wrote of Summer promenading with young Bradish—and I nearly choked on my tea with laughter. Benjamin Bradish! I confess I had quite forgotten the lad, though I do recall the whispers that his family were something of legends on the cricket pitch—his father, if memory serves, was known for scoring an unbeaten century against the Oxford gentlemen, and with considerable grace. Not a cold man, just a quiet one, I think—more comfortable with a bat than ballroom chatter. If Benjamin has inherited even half of that calm and steadiness, then Summer may have chosen wisely. Do pass along my congratulations, though I reserve the right to interrogate the fellow when I return.

Sergeant Pepper continues to astonish us all. His knowledge is not simply tactical—it is instinctual. The man moves like smoke and strikes with the precision of a surgeon. He has begun to teach the men a method of close combat drawn from Eastern practices—moves I suspect are forbidden by Geneva and frowned upon by the clergy. Yet we learn them nonetheless. For what looms ahead, we will need every ounce of skill, every flicker of cunning.

At night, under cover of the trees, we conduct drills in silence. Last eve we crept two miles undetected through German perimeter brush, halted only when Thistle—our blasted goat—took offence at a rabbit and began bleating like a theatre soprano. The enemy heard nothing, fortunately, and Thistle remains among the living (though only narrowly, thanks to Bexley's pleading). He is now considered part mascot, part alarm system.

Ah, Bexley. A man of wit and steel, grown all the more human these days under the steady influence of Miss Albright. She has settled back among us as though she had never left—her manner calm, her voice even, her humour dry enough to cut through the damp of any morning. The men no longer glance at her with unease or surprise; she has become part of our rhythm, a quiet constant like the rattle of tin cups or the sigh of the guns in the distance. Even Thistle behaves himself in her company, which is no small miracle.

As for Bexley—he watches her still, but not with the startled wonder of before. There is familiarity now, and something gentler behind it. He speaks her name less often than he thinks it, I suspect, though last night I heard laughter from the direction of the supply tent—hers mingled with his—and I pretended not to notice.

Until yesterday, none of them knew her first name. It was shouted—quite by accident—when a shell fell closer than comfort allowed. "Samantha!" Bexley cried, before even he seemed to realise he'd said it. The moment passed quickly, but not without colour in his cheeks. I said nothing, though I could not help a quiet smile. For I have known her name all along—her file crossed my desk when

I signed her transfer papers. I never spoke of it, perhaps because even secrets deserve their small dignities.

In the quiet hours, I sometimes see them still, speaking in low tones near the supply tent—ostensibly about map coordinates and cipher protocols. I've my suspicions. And I confess, I do not discourage it.

It does a man good, I think, to see affection bloom even in the soil of war.

Morale has improved. The camaraderie among the men has solidified into something more than duty—it is brotherhood. Barnes, who once wouldn't share a cigarette with his own shadow, now volunteers his rations for the younger lads. Thomson, our quiet cartographer, has taken to singing before lights out—soft, lilting melodies from the Hebrides. Even Albrecht, the German defector we took in last winter, seems at peace. He prays nightly, and we do not interrupt.

I am proud of them. Each and every one. They are not soldiers only—they are craftsmen of hope, builders of a better tomorrow, even if they may never live to see it.

We have nearly completed our final preparations. The maps are drawn, escape routes etched in our minds. Sergeant Pepper has outlined our movements down to the minute. And when the time comes, we shall strike—not for glory, but to prevent something terrible from gaining foothold.

There are whispers of a new enemy weapon. A device or installation that, if left untouched, may wreak devastation upon our lines. Samantha's intelligence aligns with Pepper's reports. Thus, we move not just as warriors—but as shields.

My dearest, as I lie here, I think of your hands. How they once brushed the snow from my coat in Hyde Park. How they turned the pages of your novels with the gentlest care. I imagine them reaching for mine when this is all over. I promise you—I shall come home. Whether limping or laughing, I shall return to you.

Until then, hold fast. Let the letters be our lifeline.

Yours, ever and always,
Wesley Anderson Crosington

August 20th, 1915
Langdon House, Kensington Square,
London

My Dearest Wesley,

Your most recent letter arrived this morning, and I read it beneath the trembling light of the drawing room window before the house had even stirred. You are often in my dreams, but never so vividly as when your words are still fresh upon the page. I pictured you beneath the trees, wrapped in shadow and resolve, writing to me while your men rested nearby. Oh, how near and far you feel in the same breath.

Thistle the goat made me laugh aloud. I cannot imagine how the creature survived conscription, yet I thank Providence daily for the strange and faithful companions war sometimes sends. It soothes me to think you are not entirely without comic relief. Promise me you'll give him a soft pat on my behalf—though do whisper to him that a rabbit is not a German soldier.

Your account of Miss Albright made me smile. How curious it must be for her—returning to your company

207

after so long, and slipping so naturally back into that strange fraternity of men and mud. I admire her composure more than I can say. It takes a rare kind of woman to command both respect and silence among soldiers.

And now that her Christian name is known—Samantha!—I cannot help but feel she has stepped out from behind the veil of mystery you wove around her. How like Bexley to be the one to uncover it, and quite by accident too! I am glad for him. You once wrote that he preferred his boots polished and his emotions buried; perhaps Miss Albright has managed to unearth something worth keeping.

I suppose there is a quiet strength in women like her—those who move unnoticed until their steadiness is most needed. In that, I see something familiar. The world may measure courage in medals and marches, but ours is often found in waiting, in enduring, and in loving across impossible distances.

Here in London, the city is humming like a hive. The newspapers speak daily of the expeditionary force in France. The name "Old Contemptibles" has caught fire, and I am told it was the Kaiser himself who dubbed them such—a slight turned into a badge of honour. The War

Office has taken to publishing casualty lists and small battlefield sketches, and I cannot help but run my fingers along the names, searching not just for yours, but for anyone I once passed in the park or knew from school.

Bethany and Kimberly joined me at the Ritz yesterday. Kimberly brought her latest beau in tow—a young man who looked like he had not yet earned the right to shave, though he quoted Shakespeare with such passion we forgave him nearly everything. Bethany, ever the diplomat, toasted to "Summer's Summer," and we all laughed as if the war were only a curtain we could close when the light grew too grim.

Summer, for her part, is positively glowing. You would be proud. Benjamin Bradish walked with her through Hyde Park last Sunday, and it caused quite the ripple. Word spread like champagne bubbles through the breakfast parlours and drawing rooms. The Bradishes are banking bluebloods, as you well know, but Benjamin is said to be a quieter soul than his kin—bookish, thoughtful, a cricketer in spirit and a gentleman in tone. He requested her company again this weekend, and though she blushed furiously, she did not say no.

I watch her, Wesley, and I see a reflection of what we once were before this cursed war. There is joy still, hidden in pockets and teacups, in the glances across supper tables and the rustle of skirts before a dance. The world has not yet burned it all away.

I pray nightly for your safety and strength—for the men who walk beside you, and the burden you now bear. I have no illusions of what lies ahead. But know that I believe in you with every breath I take.

Come home to me, Wesley. When this ends, I shall be waiting on the platform, wearing the ribbon you tied into my hair that afternoon in Kensington Gardens. And I will not let go of your hand ever again.

Yours eternally,
Savannah Langdon

London Life in Wartime

The crisp month of August in 1915 brought more than news from the front—it ushered in a delicate awakening in London's high society, as those at home attempted to carry on with grace, dignity, and their peculiar brand of controlled chaos. For Savannah Langdon, life had become a series of balancing acts: between the sorrow of absence and the duty of hosting; between late-night prayer vigils and early-morning editorial meetings.

Langdon House remained a hive of activity. Despite the war, the Langdon printing press had expanded in both reputation and responsibility. With her father recently returned from America and then taken ill shortly thereafter, Savannah had gradually stepped into a more prominent role. Though she was careful not to appear too assertive in public—lest the board of trustees grow uneasy at a woman's rising influence—behind closed doors, she had become a strategist of paper and ink. Editions rolled off the presses faster than ever, carrying with them both grim war reports and uplifting stories of heroism and community.

But it was Summer's social debut that captivated Savannah's private world.

After a splendid coming-out party only weeks prior, Summer Langdon was now officially "in society," and the courtship dances had begun in earnest. She was radiant, both in person and in spirit, though she remained somewhat torn between her newfound place among the debutantes and her love for all things intellectual. Her heart belonged to books and baby animals, and she could often be found slipping away from a tea to rescue an injured sparrow or to write a letter to a Latin scholar she admired in Florence.

Still, Summer carried herself with elegance at her first promenades, and no moment captured more attention than her walk with Benjamin Bradish through Hyde Park. Dressed in soft lilac, with white gloves and an orchid pinned at her shoulder, she looked every bit the young lady society had been expecting.

Benjamin, for his part, surprised them all. Known more as "the banker's boy," he instead demonstrated gentle humour and remarkable poise. He recited poetry, asked after Summer's love of animals, and even offered to help her visit a local veterinary hospital supporting wounded war horses. The rumour mill, of course, took this as clear intent. His name appeared twice on her next dance card—an unusually bold statement in London circles.

Back at Langdon House, Bethany and Kimberly remained Savannah's anchors. Bethany, now engaged to Greg, a surgeon overseeing medical logistics near the Belgian front, was deep into wedding plans. Every week she brought new fabric swatches and guest lists, though her eyes often drifted toward the latest telegrams. Kimberly, meanwhile, delighted in her romantic adventures. Her current flame was an aspiring playwright with no fortune and boundless dreams—a combination she found irresistible.

Between their visits, the news from the front, and the management of the Langdon press, Savannah found her hours full, her heart aching, and her spirit determined.

Wesley's letters remained her lifeline. Each word, each turn of phrase, reminded her not only of what she had lost to war—but what she hoped to gain when peace returned.

CHAPTER XXII

AUGUST 24TH, 1915
SOMEWHERE IN THE FOREST
NORTH OF YPRES, BELGIUM

My Most Cherished Savannah,

It is past midnight, and we are less than four nights from the final move. The fire is down to coals, the men speak in murmurs, and above us hangs a full and watchful moon. I write to you with trembling fingers—trembling not from fear, but from the weight of what approaches. You must forgive the blotting of ink, for I write atop my field case, with my knee as a desk and my coat as a curtain from the wind.

Sergeant Pepper has become, in only a matter of days, something of a legend among the men. It's remarkable to behold. He moves like smoke, vanishes like mist, and strikes like thunder. He has trained us in the ancient ways of stealth—tactics held sacred by warriors from East to West, honed for battle beneath the veil of darkness. We no longer speak at night. We signal with mirrors and fingers and the tilt of our heads. Each man has learned how to vanish into terrain, how to silence a footprint, how to breathe without sound.

I remembered your tales of William as a child—how he would disappear for hours in the forest behind Langdon House, returning with frogs and mud and tales of invisible enemies he had bested. That boy has become the kind of man the world rarely sees and should fear deeply if they do.

He is not alone in his transformation. These past days have drawn us close—closer, perhaps, than family. Corporal Bexley, once the picture of composure and restraint, now laughs with a looseness I've never known, as though something within him had finally learned to breathe again. Yet that lightness has dimmed of late.

Samantha's time with us has come to an end. She completed her work with the same calm precision that defined her from the first—her intellect keen, her resolve unwavering. In the final days before her departure, the camp grew subdued. The laughter of the Ghosts came softer, the clatter of cups gentler, as though all sensed that something fine and quietly necessary was leaving with her.

Tonight she departed under cover of darkness. I came upon her and Bexley at the edge of the wood, the moon caught in the folds of her greatcoat and the last light of the fire flickering behind them. They stood close, speaking little, the air thick with the weight of all they could not say. When he handed her a folded note, their hands met—not by chance, but with the deliberation of two souls holding a single instant against the pull of time.

His fingers brushed hers, then lingered, hesitant, unwilling to let go. For a long breath neither of them moved. The sounds of the camp—the shifting embers, the murmured watch-call—faded to nothing. There was only that moment: her hand in his, her eyes lifted to meet his, both of them speaking in silence the words duty would never permit. Then, with the swift resolve of someone who has already decided her fate, she slipped the note into her boot, straightened her collar, and stepped back into the shadows.

Bexley remained where she had left him, his hand still half-raised as though reluctant to believe the moment had ended. The rest of us pretended not to notice.

They have promised to write, though I suspect their truest letters were written there—in the quiet exchange of touch and courage, in the look that said what words could not.

Despite Bexley's heart, the mission must press on and we have moved into a forward position now, a sunken patch of earth near a half-destroyed chapel. Each night we advance in inches. We wear ash on our faces to dull the light of our skin, and carry branches stitched to our backs. We sleep in short turns, always with one man watching. The target lies just beyond the next rise. I cannot say much, save this: its destruction may turn the tide of this region. It is not merely a warehouse—it is a linchpin.

And so we wait, we watch, and we prepare.

I keep your letters close to my chest—literally. They rest in the same pouch as my maps, your words tucked between roads and rivers. I read them by candlelight when I can, but even when I cannot, I hear your voice in every wind. I have told the men that when I return, we shall throw a ball so grand it will echo through the halls of Parliament. I've already promised Sergeant Pepper the first waltz with the prettiest woman in London—he told me that would certainly be Kimberly, and that if she refused, he'd settle for Bethany, provided she brings her medical beau as chaperone.

And as for you, Savannah—I shall dance every dance with you, until the floorboards give out or the music ends, whichever comes last.

Our goat, Thistle, continues to be the most absurd member of the Ghosts. Last night, under strict silence, he managed to unseal a tin of pickled onions and devour them—then made such faces of disgust that we all very nearly laughed aloud. He is officially considered a security risk, and unofficially the company's spirit animal.

Dearest, should this letter find its way into your hands with nothing but silence after it, know that I walked into that valley thinking of you, hoping for you, and dreaming of what we will build when this is over.

With all that I am,
Wesley Anderson Crosington

August 28th, 1915
Langdon House, Mayfair, London

My dearest Wesley,

I write to you today by the window of my morning room, where the rain kisses the glass like a song too soft to hum. The late summer air smells of leaves already daring to turn, though the heat lingers as if reluctant to yield to the coming season. I have, since your last letter, read and reread your words until they are etched in my very breath. Oh, how I live for the quiet joy of your handwriting, and the way it slants ever so slightly when you are hurried, or deep in thought.

Word of your mission reached my ears like a prayer caught on the wind. I shall not pretend to know what danger you face nor attempt to imagine it fully—for I fear if I did, I would go mad. Instead, I trust in your skill, your courage, and the blessed favour of God Himself, who surely must have designed you for such a time as this. The name "Crosington" still causes the staff to straighten when spoken aloud, but it is your first name that makes me smile—Wesley, my Wesley, brave and brilliant.

219

Your mention of Miss Albright's departure lingered with me long after I finished your letter. I know too well the particular ache of women at war—the ones who must move through their days with measured steps and guarded hearts, who speak calmly when the world demands they weep, and love quietly when circumstance forbids any declaration. We find our courage not in grand gestures, but in constancy: in work done well, in words unsent, in feelings folded neatly away like uniforms awaiting another dawn.

If Bexley grieves her absence, I understand it. Such attachments are both peril and salvation out there; they remind you that beneath all the noise and command, you are still human. And perhaps she, too, feels the same—that her strength comes not from the walls she builds, but from what she dares to keep safe behind them.

I often think of that, my dearest—how all of us, in our own ways, are holding our hearts at arm's length, trying to keep them intact until the world allows us to open them again. Until that day comes, I shall keep mine steady, and waiting for you.

The society pages have recently caught a stir over Summer's promenading with none other than Benjamin Bradish. I must say, she's taken quite naturally to the art of courtship, even if she still quotes Latin mid-conversation and apologises to bees when she steps too near their flowers. Benjamin has written Father to request permission to call upon her again—and we all know what a second promenade means. Bethany is convinced it's destiny, Kimberly thinks Summer can do better, and I just sit here smiling like the mad matron I am not yet old enough to be.

Bethany, ever elegant in her judgments, has begun the business of choosing lace samples for her wedding dress. She has not received a letter from Greg in over ten days, and I can feel the worry beginning to bloom behind her eyes like frost on glass. She will not speak of it, but I know it lingers. Kimberly, meanwhile, is entangled in a flirtation with a gentleman who plays the violin and wears too much cologne. It is utterly scandalous and entirely delightful. I dare say she's enjoying herself far too much, which, under these heavy clouds of war, is its own quiet defiance.

As for me, the press has become my sanctuary and my burden both. Father's absence has thrust decisions into my hands, and though I often feel I am playing at authority, the staff have thus far not revolted. Our latest run went to a series of charity appeals for relief efforts in Belgium, and it feels righteous to be printing something that stirs action. I visited the main print hall two days ago, and the air was thick with ink and steam and purpose. I shall describe it in more detail below, but for now, know this: I walked the floor with my skirts tied up, speaking with the foreman as though I knew precisely what a rotary cylinder press demanded—and by God, I think I fooled them all.

Your news of Sergeant Pepper stilled my heart. William. To think of my brother by your side—I can hardly express the knot of pride and fear that formed at the base of my ribs. You shall look out for one another. You must. He was always brave—braver than me—but when we were children and he climbed trees or stormed the woods with a wooden sword, he always returned home with scraped knees and stories to make me laugh. I can only hope his stories now are gentler than his battlefield.

Write again soon, if you can. Even if it is but one word.

With my soul ever leaning toward yours,
Savannah Langdon

August 1915 – London Society, Printing, and the Rumours of Courtship

While Wesley marched silently toward his mission in the scarred fields of Belgium, Savannah Langdon moved through the grand salons and smoky press halls of wartime London—her corset tugged tighter by expectation, her heart stretched wider with longing.

The season had not yet ended in London, though it bore now the stain of war in every gown and gathering. Where once champagne had flowed like water, it now trickled in rationed sips—if at all. The Queen's charity garden parties had become quiet affairs filled with silk, somber eyes, and baskets passed for donations to hospitals, field ambulances, and refugee efforts. Savannah, flanked by Bethany and Kimberly, had recently attended one such event at Devonshire House. There, among the rhododendrons and patriotic bunting, they mingled with other young women whose sweethearts, brothers, and fathers were far away.

Bethany, though graceful as ever, carried within her the silent ache of love stretched thin by distance. Her fiancé, Gregory Hawthorne, served as a medical officer overseeing surgical supplies along the Western Front. The letters had slowed, and no one dared say why.

Kimberly, on the other hand, took to war with irreverent charm, turning every gathering into a chance for flirtation or mischief. Her current infatuation—a violinist from the Royal Academy who claimed to be descended from Paganini—had gifted her a red ribbon "charmed by music." Whether this charm extended to the battlefield, no one was certain, but it certainly had bewitched Kimberly.

Summer Langdon, meanwhile, was blooming. Her recent promenade with Benjamin Bradish was the talk of more than one garden party. The Bradishes, famed in banking and cricket alike, were a proud if reserved family. Benjamin had inherited his father's kindness and his mother's elegant posture—and, more surprisingly, a subtle charm that caught even Summer off guard. When he appeared on her dance card twice at Lady Winstone's recent assembly, tongues wagged for days. A formal courtship was not yet declared, but the gentle undercurrent of intent ran deep.

Yet it was within the ink-stained world of the press that Savannah found her truest expression. Langdon &

Sons Publishing—now run in part by a daughter—was abuzz with newsprint destined for trenches and town squares. The machines roared like dragons: rotary cylinder presses spinning fast and furious, letterpresses clacking in rhythmic precision. The foremen watched Savannah with a mixture of curiosity and respect; though few women had ever walked those aisles, she did so with a clipboard in one hand and purpose in the other.

She studied line spacing, paper stock weights, and even inquired about a new Linotype machine capable of setting whole lines of type at once. Her father's oldest compositor—Mr. Whittier—took to calling her "Miss Inkfingers" behind her back, but it was not cruel. It was affectionate. She was, in their eyes, part of the press now.

And all the while, she waited—for letters, for a name on a telegram, for the war to end, for Wesley to return.

But waiting, as Savannah well knew, was never passive. It was an act of strength. Of hope.

Of love, enduring across distance.

Chapter XXIII

September 9th, 1915
From the Edge of the Forest, Near the Ruins of Courtrai

My Dearest Savannah,

It is done.

The deed is accomplished, the powder spent, the fire extinguished, and I—though wearied, bruised, and still catching my breath—am alive to tell you of it. What we did last night may very well change the course of this theatre of war.

I scarcely know how to begin, for it seems at once the conclusion of a chapter and the birth of something altogether new.

It began under a crescent moon. We moved in silence, blackened from head to toe, each man carrying a coil of wire or a satchel charge, each one of us drilled like clockwork thanks to Sergeant Pepper's training. We had been watching the enemy's installation for nearly three weeks, mapping their schedules, counting their deliveries, and noting the peculiar terrain surrounding it. The target was a deeply fortified munitions relay centre disguised beneath a crumbling estate—a former vineyard, now pulsing with the lifeblood of war.

They called it *Schloss der Zerstörung*—Castle of Destruction.

Pepper had uncovered critical intelligence suggesting the site housed experimental war gas and a prototype weapons system, a so-called "Doomsday Device" built to flood trenches with poisonous vapours in one fell breath. A cruel, indiscriminate thing. A monstrosity of modern design. If deployed, it could wipe out entire regiments in minutes.

The air that night smelled of iron and wet stone. I led the first team. Bexley shadowed me, carrying the blast map. Pepper went with the second team to the rear entrance, guiding the new men with an almost supernatural grace. When the signal came—an owl's call—we moved. There was no room for error. Our hands remembered what our minds could not afford to think.

I cannot recount every moment, nor would I wish to. There was smoke, shouting, and the awful groaning of the great machine being brought to ruin. But I will tell you this: when the explosion came, it lit the sky as if dawn had arrived early. A column of fire twenty feet high shook the heavens. We had laid our charges well.

And then—the gas began to leak.

For a breathless moment we believed we had all perished. The wind shifted. But by Providence and God's hand, the foul mist rolled back toward the enemy lines. We had made our escape through the south corridor and climbed into the old drainage culverts, dragging two injured men with us. I do not know how we were not caught. I only know we were meant to survive.

We destroyed their terror weapon. The Allies cheered across the line. Word has travelled like fire in a dry wood. We are no longer mere shadows—we are Crosington's Ghosts in legend now.

Bexley announced it to us this morning, there by the fire as the mist still clung to the ground. He tried for nonchalance, but his grin gave him away before he'd finished the first sentence. He means to propose to Miss Samantha Albright the moment he's home again. There was a hush for half a heartbeat, and then the men cheered—real, unguarded laughter that chased away the chill better than the coffee ever could.

There was excitement in Bexley's voice, yes, but also the unmistakable tremor of a man who knows he's wagering his whole heart. Between sips of tea he confessed his one great fear—that Miss Albright, with her steady eyes and formidable intellect, might take the news as an infraction of some secret regulation. "If she says no," he said, "I expect to be court-martialed for insubordination." The camp roared, and even I had to admit the image of her delivering the sentence was not entirely implausible.

Yet beneath the laughter, there was something else—a brightness, a kind of hope we haven't felt in months. It lingers still.

As the dawn broke and the earth settled after such momentous news, a courier arrived from the War Office. The message, sealed in green wax, bore news I could scarce believe: I am being summoned home.

Savannah, they have requested my return to serve as an advisor to the Committee of Imperial Defence, a position of grave honour, born of the Ghosts' success and my family's legacy. I must return to Parliament, and—at last—to you. It is not only my military achievements they cite, but my inheritance. With Father gone, the family's steel and railroad empire must not fall into disrepair.

And so I write this letter from the field with one boot already cleaned and a new uniform waiting in a parcel. It will not be long now.

Sergeant Pepper will remain behind, returning to his deep-cover unit to continue the fight. I have come to trust him with my very life. He clasped my hand this morning and said, "Go home, Crosington. The world will need you after this."

I have hinted at it for many moons, but now I may speak more freely: there is a secret I must share with you when I return. A gift. Something my father hid away for us before he passed. I will not say where, but you already know the hints: America, behind a house, beneath an old red building, under the floorboards, beside a tree. We will go together and find it, when all of this is done.

Until then, I remain your ever-devoted,
Wesley Anderson Crosington

September 15th, 1915
Langdon House, London

My Most Beloved Wesley,

I scarcely know how to begin.

Your letter arrived this morning, carried in the trembling hands of our footman, who, though trained in discretion, betrayed all when he cried out, "It is from him, Miss Savannah—it is from Mr. Crosington!" I did not scold him. I could not, for I was already tearing the wax and nearly fainting with joy.

I sat in the breakfast room for the reading of it, and by the end, my tea had gone entirely cold, and so had my fingers. And yet my heart—oh, my darling, my heart is warmer than it has been in months. You are alive. You are victorious. You are coming home.

What glory you and your brave companions have accomplished! I could scarcely breathe at the thought of your peril. That monstrous installation—what name did you say? *Schloss der Zerstörung*? How terribly poetic and grotesque. I picture it rising from the ground like some mad cathedral, born of hate and smoke. And yet you—you have undone it. You and Sergeant Pepper, and Bexley, and the noble Ghosts. I wept at the thought of you crawling through gas and ruin. I wept again when I read of your survival. You were always meant to walk through fire and come out clean on the other side.

And now, they call you home. I daresay it is just in time, for I do not know how much longer my heart could bear your absence. You shall return not only to your family and your titles, but to me. To us. To a future we have only whispered of in the quiet dark.

The Committee of Imperial Defence! My dear, I believe that is the very council upon which Churchill himself once advised. What an honour! They shall not know what to do with your wit and steel-eyed purpose, but I suspect they shall adjust quickly. I have long known you were made for more than the shadows of war.

Your account of Bexley's announcement made me laugh aloud—I could almost hear the cheers from your campfire echoing across the Channel. How marvellous to think of him, usually so composed, now undone by the thought of a proposal! I should like to have seen his face when he confessed his fear of Miss Albright's reply. You must tell him that no woman of sound mind could refuse such a man; though, given her formidable air, I can understand his caution. If she does decline, I daresay she will do so with perfect decorum—before promptly convening a tribunal to reprimand him for his presumption.

What a strange and lovely thing, to hear of love still daring to bloom amid so much uncertainty. It fills me with a kind of hope I scarcely dare to name. Tell Bexley that I shall be waiting eagerly for news, and that when he and Miss Albright do marry, I expect a proper invitation—and a glass of champagne poured in her honour. In their happiness, I see a glimmer of our own, waiting patiently for its turn.

I do not yet know what you have planned for this gift you mention—the secret that's teased me across a dozen letters. But I hold to your hints with great care. An old red building, under the floorboards, beside a tree...in America. I do not know what lies waiting, but I know it shall be a great gift indeed.

I long for the moment your train arrives. I shall wear the green dress—the one from that night we first danced beneath the crystal chandeliers. Do you remember? You asked if I would ever learn to waltz properly. You made a fine tutor, as I recall.

Until you arrive, I shall busy myself with everything and nothing, and carry your letter folded in my bodice like a sacred charm. London seems brighter already.

Ever yours,
Savannah Langdon

September 16th, 1915 – London Society, Secrets, and the Shimmer of Anticipation

The letter from Wesley Crosington arrived not just to Savannah Langdon, but to the whole of London society, in spirit if not in fact. For when Savannah received word of his victory and imminent return, the ripple of joy it sent through her circle was as strong as any telegram.

Bethany burst into the Langdon drawing room not two hours after, demanding details. She wore her usual rose silk, her gloves askew and her cheeks flushed from the autumn wind. "Tell me everything!" she squealed, before even greeting the butler. Kimberly trailed behind her, dragging in two parcels of pastries and half a bottle of elderberry cordial, claiming it was "for the nerves."

The three girls spent the entire afternoon lounging on the floor, reading Wesley's letter aloud, paragraph by paragraph, pausing between sentences to interpret its hidden meanings. Bethany, ever the romantic, declared that a man who writes of crawling through enemy tunnels is "a poet or a madman," and probably both. Kimberly, more practical, asked if Bexley was single and if he looked better now with the war beard or before, when he was clean-shaven.

Savannah, of course, said nothing on the subject of beards.

Word had already reached their little circle that Bexley and the mysterious Samantha Albright—rumoured to be a war office attaché—had begun writing. Bethany, who fancied herself the queen of wartime romance, pronounced it "impossibly gallant," and had already begun plotting their hypothetical wedding menu.

Meanwhile, young Summer Langdon was beside herself with joy. Her presentation into society had barely cooled, and yet Benjamin Bradish, heir to the Bradish banking fortune, had already sent word that he would like to promenade with her in the park next Thursday. There was talk of plum tarts and the return of her favourite gloves from the cleaners. Savannah and the girls helped her rehearse polite conversation starters ("Do you enjoy Milton?") and the more casual, fashionable variations ("Have you read the latest essays by Shaw?").

As for the printing empire—Langdon Press & Co.—the war had only made the business more demanding. Paper was scarce. Ink rationed. But their influence grew daily. Savannah took to the linotype floor herself on occasion, her gloves off and her hair tied in a ribbon, learning the workings of the mighty press machines and the rhythm of their endless dance. The workers respected her. Some adored her. And though no formal title passed to her, it was understood that Miss Langdon's word was gospel when it came to the editorial line. She walked now through the halls her father built with a steady grace and a quiet fire.

Yet even amid the demands of paper and type, dances and dresses, Savannah found herself slipping more and more into dreams of New York. Wesley had spoken of it, albeit cryptically. The red building. The oak tree. The floorboards. Her father had once said, "That boy will never dig a hole without planting a story in it." She could not wait to discover what seeds he had buried.

And so London turned with the slow elegance of a clockwork waltz. The war carried on, distant thunder in France. The Langdons carried on, with their tea and their presses. And Savannah Langdon, for all her poise and polish, for all her wit and command, sat by the window that evening and whispered aloud the words she had waited so long to say:

"He is coming home."

CHAPTER XXIV

FROM THE HAND OF WESLEY
ANDERSON CROSINGTON, EN
ROUTE TO LONDON
SOMEWHERE PAST YORK,
OCTOBER 1915

My Dearest Savannah,

This letter I write not from the trenches nor under
the solemn glow of the moon in some foreign field, but
from the rhythmic comforts of a railway carriage swaying
gently toward home. The war—our war—is behind me
now. At least, the part I was summoned to play. The
guns, for me, have fallen silent. Yet even now, I hear
echoes in the whistle of this train.

I would that you could see what I see from this
window: green fields returning to their colours, trees
reclaiming their golds and rusts, and English mist
crawling like velvet across the hillocks. They remind me
of everything we fought to protect—and everything I
now return to.

We were victorious, Savannah. The operation succeeded. The machine of death they sought to unleash was dismantled, its creators scattered like smoke in the wind. Sergeant Pepper—your brother William—stood beside me as we stormed the final installation. It was his intelligence, his courage, and his uncanny skill under darkness that allowed our Ghosts to thread through the enemy's steel-twined defences. He remains behind, of course—too proud, too noble, to leave the fight before its true end. I suspect the legend of Sergeant Pepper will grow, as it rightly should.

As for Bexley—he is alive, whole, and grinning like a fool. He carries letters in his coat from Samantha Albright, and has begun referring to her as *his north star*. I believe he intends to propose the moment he sets foot on English soil again. There will be another wedding, Savannah, and we shall attend it side-by-side, if fate is kind.

But allow me, before I return, to tell you—not of battles, not of bombs—but of the men I knew, the bonds we forged, and the way they shaped me.

When first I took command of Crosington's Ghosts, I was but a titled son with a sabre, a mind full of ideals and a heart still green. I believed in honour, yes, but I scarcely knew the price of it. Now I do. I have seen it bought with blood and silence, with the last breaths of boys who will never grow old, who called for their mothers or sang old pub songs as the dark took them.

But amid that sorrow bloomed a rare and holy thing: brotherhood. I came to know men whose hands were calloused from farms, from shipyards, from mines and mills—and whose courage burned no less bright than a general's star. There was Triggs, who once repaired looms in Leeds, and now repaired souls with a well-timed joke. There was Hensley, who could strip a Vickers gun blindfolded and still made time to teach me proper Yorkshire swearing. And Ewan—sweet, silent Ewan—who never spoke of home, but carved a tiny likeness of his daughter into a cartridge case and carried it like a talisman.

They taught me leadership not by rule or rank, but by trust, by truth, by shared hardship. They showed me that the measure of a man is not in medals, but in the quiet sacrifices made for those beside him.

And so I return to you not merely as a soldier, nor even as a son newly burdened with title and empire—but as a man reshaped by fire. The sorrow I carry now, I carry gladly, for it makes the joy I long for with you all the more vivid.

And I *do* long for you, Savannah.

I think of you constantly—your wit, your letters, your fierce heart. You have been my thread back to the world, my anchor and my light. I've seen things, love, that make beauty more precious, more urgent. And I find myself counting the minutes until I see your face again—your real face, not the one I've etched so stubbornly into memory.

When next I write, it shall not be from war, nor from railway, but from your side. If all goes to plan, I shall be stepping down from this train into the arms of the woman I have loved since that first day in London.

Until then—
Yours eternally,
Wesley

From the hand of Miss Savannah Langdon
Grosvenor Square, London
Fall, 1915

My Dearest Wesley,

I scarcely know how to begin this letter, for my hands tremble as they write—not from fear or sorrow, but from the exquisite joy of knowing you are coming home. *Home*, Wesley. Not in spirit, not in hopes, but in body, in breath, in all the parts of you I have longed for through every moonlit window and echoing corridor.

I read your letter three times, and then again by lamplight when the house had gone still. Each word—your words—felt like a knock on the door of my soul. I closed my eyes and could see you there, riding that train through the Yorkshire hills, your thoughts full of duty, but your heart, perhaps, full of me.

Oh, Wesley... I knew you would return, though there were nights I doubted my courage. I told myself you would emerge not just alive, but forged anew—sharper, wiser, softer in all the right places. And so you have. In your letter I saw not just the man I fell in love with, but the man the world will now reckon with: tempered, tested, triumphant.

I know too well the price of such transformation. I wept, reading of your brothers in arms—Triggs, Hensley, Ewan. Names that were never inked in the papers, never toasted in drawing rooms, and yet who gave more than most could fathom. Please tell me their stories again when we are old, that I might honour them with tears and remembrance.

Your description of Sergeant Pepper nearly sent me flying out the front door in pride. My brother, grown into a legend before my very eyes. I suspect when I next see him, I shall find more steel than boy in his stance, but the same riverbank smile beneath it all.

As for Bexley—what a dear fool. I cannot wait to see the way his ears turn red when Samantha Albright appears at the altar. And I *do* hope she wears something utterly improper. Perhaps red. Bethany insists it would be too scandalous, but Kimberly and I are in agreement: this world could use more scandal if it's born of love.

Now, for the truth I've whispered into pillows but never dared write aloud: I have missed you more than any language allows. I missed the tilt of your brow when you tease me, the way you sip tea far too slowly, and the quiet gravity you bring into every room. London has felt like a stage awaiting your entrance.

I shall be waiting at the platform.

Return to me soon, my Wesley. Let us put down the swords of war and take up the pen of peace. Let us write a new chapter—not in ink, but in sunlit mornings and shared pillows and warm firelight where no bombs may reach us.

Ever Yours,
Savannah

The Reunion at Paddington

The station was choked with steam and laughter. Paddington had never known such a day, for though soldiers returned with some regularity now, few returned to quite the same reception as Wesley Anderson Crosington.

Savannah stood perfectly still beneath the iron awning, a small leather glove crushed in her hand, and the green dress from the night they first danced, it clung to her frame like an echo of that long-ago ball. Her hat sat smartly atop her flowing hair, the ribbon he'd given her at Kensington Gardens tied in a perfect bow. Her cheeks were painted by the natural blush of hope, and her eyes—those grey-green lanterns—scanned every train car with a desperation masked only by pride.

The doors clattered open. And then, he was there.

He stepped down in full uniform, taller somehow, his shoulders broad with honour, his boots worn from command. He looked about him once, blinking into the sunlight, and then—

He saw her.

The crowd around them blurred. Not even the porters remained distinct. He walked to her slowly, each footfall deliberate. No salute, no bow, no word.

He dropped to one knee.

From his coat pocket, he pulled a small velvet pouch. Within it lay a ring—simple, elegant, forged of family gold melted down from a piece of his late father's pocket watch. Set within it: a single oval sapphire, pale and soft, like a pool of light at dusk.

Wesley held the ring with both hands up to Savannah and he looked up, deep into her eyes.

"Your heart, my love, has been my only home since I left you," he said softly, "I have known no rest, no peace, but in the memory of your voice. If you'll have me, Savannah Langdon, I shall build with you a kingdom and give you all my tomorrows."

She did not speak. She wept. The sort of tears that belong to springtime and homecomings.

Her answer, whispered against his brow, was yes.

As the steam rose once more and the train pulled away, Wesley stood and wrapped his arms about her. Behind them, the gaslights flickered on, casting long shadows like future memories across the stone.

London's bells rang out that night in triumph.

But beneath the floorboards of an old red barn in New York, something else stirred—the promise of the next great chapter. For the war had ended for one man, and begun for another. And love, that indomitable fire, burned brighter still.

The End.

THE REAL HISTORICAL EVENTS MIRRORED IN - WRITTEN WITH LOVE, SURROUNDED BY WAR

The Christmas Truce of 1914

Mirrored in: Wesley's Letter

Real event: On Christmas Eve and Christmas Day, 1914, British and German troops on the Western Front ceased fire, emerged from their trenches, and met in No Man's Land to exchange small gifts, sing carols, and in some places even play football (soccer).

249

Historical context: This spontaneous act of humanity was not sanctioned by high command but spread through various sectors. It's seen as a moment of peace amidst brutal war.

Reflected in the book: Wesley and his unit experience a similar moment of peace, sharing a Christmas meal and temporary ceasefire.

Life in the Trenches

Mirrored throughout: Wesley's Letters

Real events: Soldiers endured horrific conditions—mud, lice, trench foot, constant shellfire, and psychological trauma ("shell shock").

Details included:

Daily routines of digging, waiting, and shelling

Cramped dugouts, rations, cold nights

Camaraderie, song, poetry, shared food and humor (e.g., Bexley's harmonica)

Reflected in the book: The rhythm of trench life is captured in vivid detail—emphasizing the bond between soldiers like Bexley, Emery, and Wesley.

Introduction of New War Machines

Mirrored in: Letter X and beyond

Real innovations:

Tanks: First used in the Battle of the Somme (1916); called "landships" at the time—slow, mechanically unreliable, but terrifying.

Flamethrowers: First used by the Germans, creating panic in Allied lines.

Airplanes: Reconnaissance early on, then dogfights; WWI pilots often flew without parachutes in open-cockpit biplanes.

Reflected in the book: Wesley's commentary on these machines is filled with awe, skepticism, and concern.

The London War Effort

Mirrored in: Savannah's Letters

Real events:

Women organized fundraisers, charity balls, and sewing circles for the troops.

The British Red Cross and Voluntary Aid Detachment (VAD) grew in prominence.

Society girls helped in hospitals, war kitchens, and ambulance units.

Reflected in the book: Savannah, along with her friends Bethany and Kimberly, plans social events to fundraise for medical supplies and soldiers' welfare.

Debutante Culture and Coming Out Balls

Mirrored in: Author Narratives after Savannah's letters

Real events: Young aristocratic women were formally presented in society through debutante balls. These events were highly ritualized with dance cards, promenades in Hyde Park, and parlor etiquette.

Reflected in the book: Savannah's younger sister Summer has a formal "coming out" party with traditional etiquette, dance styles, and courtship rituals. Benjamin Bradish's interest is noted by his repeat presence on her dance card.

The Printing Press and Media Influence

Mirrored in: Savannah's involvement in her family's publishing house

Real events: WWI was one of the first wars heavily shaped by mass media.

Newspapers shaped public opinion and morale.

Powerful families like the Langdons (fictional) mirror real publishing magnates like the Harmsworth brothers (Lord Northcliffe) who controlled the Daily Mail and The Times.

Reflected in the book: Savannah plays an increasingly strategic role in wartime messaging, carefully threading emotion, patriotism, and truth.

Elite Military Units & Espionage (Crosington's Ghosts & Sergeant Pepper) - Special Forces of WWI

Mirrored in: Crosington's Ghosts (fictional), inspired by:

Royal Naval Division (RND)

British Commandos (formally post-WWI but tactics existed earlier)

Lovat Scouts and Arditi (Italian) used stealth, camouflage, and guerilla tactics.

Real tactics:

Night raids, wire cutting, and reconnaissance

Camouflaged movements through No Man's Land

Reflected in the book: Wesley leads "Crosington's Ghosts," a covert elite group trained in stealth and unconventional warfare.

Military Intelligence & Female Spies

Mirrored in: Samantha Albright's role

Real events:

Women served in secret as intelligence agents, codebreakers, and couriers.

The Secret Intelligence Service (SIS) (later MI6) existed at the time.

Louise de Bettignies, a French spy, and Edith Cavell, a nurse who helped soldiers escape, were famous figures.

Reflected in the book: Samantha Albright is a brave and unconventional intelligence officer who aids Wesley's team and develops a romance with Bexley.

Historical Military Installations

Mirrored in: The Great Mission

Based on: Real Allied efforts to destroy:

German supply depots

Artillery emplacements

Critical rail yards or zeppelin hangars

Reflected in the book: The Ghosts conduct a special operation to cripple a major enemy installation, turning the tide for their sector.

Government Roles and Legacy - *Advisory Positions in Parliament*

Mirrored in: Wesley's call home

Real event:

The Committee of Imperial Defence (CID) was the real wartime advisory body that shaped British military and colonial strategy.

Members included former officers, ministers, and trusted lords.

Reflected in the book: Wesley is summoned home to advise Parliament in the CID after the success of his mission—reflecting his rising influence.

BOOK II - PREVIEW

Written with Love, Hearts of Ink and Iron

Book II of the Written with Love Saga

Winter, 1915.

The frost lingers over London, the war rages on in France, and yet—amidst uniforms and telegrams, strategy rooms and soirées—a long-awaited union prepares to bloom.

Lady Savannah Langdon will soon become Lady Crosington.

Sir Wesley Crosington, once a soldier in the mud of Béthune, now walks the marbled halls of Parliament, appointed to Britain's Committee of Imperial Defence—a secretive group guiding the fate of the Empire as the Great War stretches on.

261

Their wedding is to be the quiet anchor in a world unraveling.

But even before the flowers fade, their journey takes flight across the Atlantic.

In America, a new frontier calls.

As the Crosington Transcontinental Railway begins laying track through frozen timber and gold-rush towns, Savannah dares to expand her family's London press into the bold, brash West. But the Gilded Age is transforming into something far more ruthless. In New York's glittering parlours and on the wide, wind-swept plains, they'll face rivals, robber-barons, and the politics of a nation caught between isolation and war.

He builds empires of steel.

She builds empires of ink.

Together, they'll shape a new world—if the old one doesn't tear them apart first.

From the embers of Europe to the promise of the West... the saga continues.